Far Above Rubies

Far Above Rubies

Anne-Marie Vukelic

ROBERT HALE · LONDON

ISBN 978-0-7090-9053-3

Robert Hale Limited
Clerkenwell House
Clerkenwell Green
London EC1R 0HT

www.halebooks.com

Typeset in 11/14¼pt Palatino
by Derek Doyle & Associates, Shaw Heath
Printed in Great Britain by the MPG Books Group,
Bodmin and King's Lynn

AUTHOR'S NOTE

I hope that my readers will forgive me where they find that, in my earnest desire to capture the spirit of Catherine Dickens, and to tell her story, I have on occasions departed from known facts, or dramatized them.

At the close of the novel there is an appendix which is intended to enlighten the reader as to which of the chapters are based upon well-documented accounts of the life of Charles and Catherine Dickens, and those which have sprung purely from my own imagination. In addition, it clarifies where dates, names and places may have been changed or added to suit the purpose of a novel.

ACKNOWLEDGEMENTS

My thanks go first to my husband, Steve, without whose loving support I could never have found the time to write this novel. Additionally, I am grateful to Mr Roger Flavell BA (Oxon) for his invaluable suggestions and for the sharing of endless resources; to Professor Francis O'Gorman for insightful advice pertaining to synopses, and to my nephew, Michael Carter, for being a sounding board at the submission stage. Miss Eleanor Carter gave of her time to read the first completed draft of *Far Above Rubies* for which I am most appreciative, and I am grateful to my father, Mr George Carter, for his assistance with the title. Thank ... Richard, for being who you are, and to my boys, Jon-Marc and Alexander for making me so proud.

CHAPTER ONE

11 June 1870
Gad's Hill Place, Kent

I often wondered how I had arrived at the person that I was now, the person that I had become, and I have asked myself many times, 'is it circumstances that form a person, or does a person form his own set of circumstances'?

In the beginning, I was not at all as I am now – or was I? – too many years have passed by for me to remember now, but after his death I never ceased reflecting: if a man desiring a quiet and obedient wife finds that when she becomes that which he desires, his creation disappoints him – who is to blame? The woman for displeasing her husband, or the man who has made her what she is now?

26 December 1834
18 York Place, Chelsea

'Alice! It is nearly seven o'clock and the little ones are not yet in bed.'

My mother's voice held a note of hysteria in addressing the maid, which was her custom whether the emergency was real or imagined. 'The guests will be arriving soon: please will you hurry?'

Situated at the end of an elegant curved terrace, our house had been in need of much repair when Papa had bought it, and hence he had secured it at reduced price, but now he was the well-respected editor of the *Evening Chronicle* and our home reflected his elevated station in life. It was Boxing Day and Papa, who was a keen cellist, was holding a musical evening for a small circle of his talented and amusing friends. My sister, Mary, and I delighted in such evenings, and while Mary loved to practice her conversation, I preferred to stand on the edge and watch the guests with occupied interest. Papa's parties were a wonderful opportunity to stay up late, observing the adult world of which we would soon be a part.

The bedroom was in complete disarray, dresses were strewn across the bed, shoes tumbled from the wardrobe and no matter where I looked, I could not find my sapphire ear-rings. Even little Georgina became caught up in the excitement and I became hot with impatience as we bumped heads in her attempt to try on my jewellery before her bedtime.

'Georgie! If you insist upon bouncing on that bed any longer, I shall chase you from the room!' I snapped.

In the rumpus of confusion, Mary sensed my frustration and she carefully unclipped the jewellery from her own ears and held out her hand.

'Here, take mine, Catherine,' she smiled.

It was an act that typified her nature: as a child, Mary had always shared her toys, played the games that other children wished to play and, when slighted, forgave all in a moment. Mary always told the truth, and saw the good in everyone. In short, through my sister's eyes, the world was a beautiful place. I, however, had a hot temper. I knew it only too well and found that I could not help but be hasty, even when I tried not to be.

Among the guests that evening were Mr John Black, editor of the *Morning Chronicle*, an intellectually minded liberal and an accomplished raconteur, Sir John Easthope, the proprietor of the aforementioned, Mr Thomas Anderson, an actor who frequently trod the boards at the Queen's Theatre in Tottenham Street,

Doctor and Mrs Francis Bell, the family physician and his wife, and Mrs Elizabeth George, a talented pianist and soprano soloist.

Mary and I surveyed ourselves in the looking-glass before going downstairs to join the party. My dark hair and heavy-lidded blue eyes were much admired, I knew, but Mary's delicate features and neat figure were also drawing attention now that she was sixteen.

The room was alive with animated conversation. Mr Black and Sir John sipped at their sherry and discussed their newspaper circulation figures. Mama conversed with Dr Bell's wife about the success of her Christmas charity work, and Mrs George warmed up her vocal chords and practised her scales on the pianoforte. After greeting the guests I stood by a half-open window, glad of the cooling air in a room full of people.

I was suddenly startled by the sound of a tapping upon the window pane, and turned to see the boyish features of a young man, his face pressed close against it. He pointed to the room and mouthed the words, 'Let – me – in.' I looked about for Papa, not at all sure what to do, when the tapping began again. The young man repeated his muted request and I threw open the window in a bid to ask him to leave; but, with the nimblest of movements, he seized the opportunity and jumped right into the room.

He was dressed in a sailor's outfit and, as no one had appeared to notice his arrival, he gave a loud cough. Satisfied that he had gained the attention he sought, he announced, 'Ladies and Gentlemen, I give you the hornpipe!' and he began to dance with sustained vigour. When he had finished, he threw open the window, jumped out, and was gone.

A few minutes later, the door opened and in walked the very same young man, dressed in his tail coat. He walked around the room, saying, 'How do you do?' and shaking hands as if he had never been here in his life before. When he saw all our puzzled faces, he roared with delight at his own tomfoolery, and I was thankful the guests did likewise. I was most grateful that everyone saw the joke as I felt quite perplexed by his outrageous behaviour.

Papa introduced him to us all as Charles Dickens, and it appeared that my father had employed him both as a reporter and to write some sketches for the *Evening Chronicle*. I must admit that I didn't know what to make of such a young man and a man he was, being four years older than myself. I watched as he talked with ease to those around him, and observed how quickly he endeared himself by means of his interesting conversation and playful humour. His manner of speaking was rapid and full of enthusiasm.

'Gentleman, let me tell you about a most remarkable case I am reporting upon at the local magistrate's court, that of a Mr Samuel Galloway, who was arrested for causing a disturbance in the City. The poor, deluded soul believed himself to be the King's brother and wished to be recognized as such!'

I stood very quietly on the edge of the group, thinking I had been listening to Mr Dickens discourse completely unnoticed by him, when suddenly he swivelled abruptly upon his heels, turned his head and addressed me directly.

'Do you know, little miss, the fellow was so convincing that when he left the courtroom, some of the witnesses lifted their caps and made a low bow!'

He roared his infectious laugh again, and I could not help but smile.

Later, as Mary and I lay in bed, talking over the evening's events, I asked her whether she had noticed Mr Dickens with his vibrant personality, his large brown eyes and his soft wavy hair. She replied dreamily that one could not fail to have missed him and that she was decidedly in love with him. We both giggled, but as Mary fell asleep I wondered why I felt such an unexpected prick of jealousy at her words.

After that, the dazzling Mr Dickens became a regular visitor to our home and I was pleased and thankful to observe that he always used the front door from then on. I realized that, as he spoke enthusiastically to my father about his work, and laughed out loud at Mary's constant chatter, his eyes rested often and longingly upon me, and although I felt shy, I found that my feelings for him were growing.

On 7 February, Charles celebrated his twenty-third birthday, and Mary and I were invited to attend a party at his lodgings in Furnival's Inn. I was disappointed to find that they were situated at the end of a narrow, dog-legged alleyway which opened out onto a dismal courtyard; but my disappointment was quickly extinguished by Charles's enthusiastic welcome.

'Come in! Come in! Come in!' and he bounded up the stairs ahead of us. He accompanied us around the room and introduced us to his other guests, until finally he came to the last two gentlemen, who appeared to be conversing intensely over legal matters.

'Ladies, may I introduce you to my good friend, Mr John Forster?'

The serious-looking young man nodded at myself and Mary in turn with the formality of an elder statesman, and Charles winked at us with an air of mischief, as if to acknowledge the humour of his friend's pomposity.

'And this is Mr Thomas Mitten, a clerk at the courts, he points me in the direction of all of the most interesting cases to report on, don't you, Mitten?'

Mr Mitten nodded cheerfully and then began to regale us with tales of legal cases both humorous and alarming. The evening progressed with such high-spirited dancing and music that I hardly noticed the gloominess of Charles's humble accommodation and, when I had not the energy to match his own, he whirled Mary around the room instead.

The next day I wrote to my cousin Elizabeth and told her how, in a quieter moment, Charles had led me to believe that he wished us to enter into an ongoing courtship; however, as I sealed the letter I wondered why it was that I was filled with a nagging uncertainty. Charles was both gentlemanly and pleasant, and Papa assured me that he had a great future ahead of him if his success matched his ambition. So why was I troubled by doubts? Because at times, I noticed how Charles seemed to enjoy Mary's company more than mine and, worse still, he would become strangely distant and preoccupied with work so that I felt that he was not giving me the first place in his attentions. But all the family loved him so: Mary continued to dote on him and showered him with gifts, little Georgina climbed onto his lap whenever she got a chance, and Mama believed that he would become every bit as accomplished as Papa. So I realized that I must lay my doubts to rest and think how blessed I was that he should set his intentions upon me.

Three months later, at a most unexpected moment, he asked me to marry him. We had been listening to Papa play the cello, when he had leaned close and whispered nervously, 'Kate, I have something to ask you. Would you find it too intolerable to become the wife of an impoverished writer?'

The sudden proposal stunned me for a moment and then I clasped his hand in fervent affirmation. 'No, my love, I wouldn't.' I laughed with delight. 'That is, I mean to say, yes, yes I will!'

He put a finger to his lips and motioned that I should let my father finish playing.

'Then let it be so,' he whispered, squeezing my hand in return.

The proposal had been all the more surprising for only the week before I feared that I had lost him for good, when he wrote and admonished me sternly for my hasty temper. It was true that whenever he was too busy with his work to see me that I would become moody and petulant the next time we were together. But I had not wanted to lose him and, having been reproved, had promised that I would endeavour to become a more placid and undemanding love in the future. It appeared that he had forgiven me after all and so I too could forgive him anything, as long as he would assure me of his steadfastness.

As if in answer to my worries, Charles took up lodgings in Selwood Terrace, a row of houses just north of Fulham Road and

only a short walk from our home in York Place. It had a pleasant
outlook and was much brighter than Furnival's Inn had been,
and I hoped that it was here that we would begin our married
life together. Mary was excited to see it, too, and presented
Charles with a silver inkwell for his desk.

'Lor', Mary, what a capital gift!' he exclaimed with pleasure
and swung her round, embracing her warmly. 'How is it that
you always seem to know just what I need, and when I need it?
You are the cleverest little lady that I ever knew.'

'I think that it is because we are of one mind, and so alike in
many ways,' she laughed, admiration shining in her eyes.

I tried not to show it, but their growing friendship sat uneasily
with me and I felt jealous again. Mary was animated in a way
that I was not and I could see that Charles delighted in her easy
company. But I reminded myself that I was the one that he called
'my dearest Kate', *I* the one who would be his wife and *I* who
would be his unfailing support. Mary would have to find her
own suitor.

CHAPTER TWO

June 1835
Selwood Terrace, Fulham

The summer was a gloriously happy one as I spent many hours in Charles's company chaperoned by Mary. We breakfasted each morning at his rooms in Selwood Terrace and I was glad that Charles had now moved closer, so that I would not have to travel through the dismal tangle of the streets of Holborn. I took no delight in side-stepping the muddy gutters and was pleased to see my love in happier surroundings.

In an endeavour to introduce me to a passion of his, Charles took Mary and me to an evening at the Theatre Royal in Rochester. It was not at all a grand place, as the name might suggest, but a quaint little country theatre which smelt of lamp oil and sawdust. However, when the curtain lifted I noticed how Charles's face lit up and radiated vitality, his expressions ever mobile and changing as the performance unfolded. He roared with laughter at the awkward acting and threadbare costumes, and seemed to forget entirely the cares of his working life. Watching him intently, his eyes alive with joy, I knew that I could not love him more than I did at that very moment.

On the way home, Mary talked excitedly and, with a slight skip in her step, hung onto Charles's arm. I looked at her fingers as they clasped and caressed the folds of his coat sleeve and I bristled with irritation.

'Gracious, Mary!' I snapped. 'Do you have to chatter so? I am sure that Charles is tired and only wishes to enjoy the peace of the evening while we walk.'

Mary looked like a whipped child and, her cheery disposition dulled, fell into a solemn silence. Charles said nothing, but I felt his disapproval keenly. How could he know that I wanted nothing more than to be alone with him? I could not help but wish that Mary would in certain circumstances disappear.

As if providence heard my wish, Mary fell ill a few days later and I found her one morning full of a terrible cold. Immediately I regretted my selfishness. Sat up in bed, her face wet with perspiration, she reassured me, 'I am quite all right, dear Sister, a few days in bed and I shall find myself quite restored to good health in no time at all.'

Mary had been accompanying me each morning to Charles's lodgings to carry out any errands that he had been too busy to attend to. Now, I was placed in a difficult position: with Mary indisposed I could not in all conscience go alone, yet surely it would not matter this once. After all Charles would not be there, he was working intensely at present, so did he not need a helping hand more that ever? I put on my bonnet decisively and, seeing me do so, a look of concern fell across Mary's face.

'Catherine, you won't be going to Selwood Terrace alone, will you? To be seen going in unchaperoned, you know it wouldn't be proper.'

'Of course, I won't,' I lied, with a toss of my head. 'I will take the ink that Charles has asked for and deliver it into the hands of his landlady. I shall be back in no time at all.' Reassured Mary settled herself back into her pillows.

Leaving home, I made the short walk to Selwood Terrace. Carts and wagons crammed with baskets passed me by, taking the road that led to the City and the weekday market. The day was hot and, consequently, when I arrived, the door to Charles's lodgings was ajar. I could hear the landlady's voice coming from the back of the house, 'That's three shillings and sixpence you owe me, Mr Wossal, and I will be obliged if you settle your debts today, or I will be asking you to move out!'

Leaving her to attend to her business, I stepped quietly up the stairs to Charles's room and took out the key that he had given for my and Mary's use. I unlocked the door, and a sense of excitement overtook me – it would be almost like being alone with him, surrounded by his things and the familiar scent that was his. I walked about the room running my fingertips lightly over his possessions and smiled. I crossed the room to his desk to leave the bottle of ink I had brought, and it was then that I was struck by the precise orderliness of everything: it was quite strange and in complete contrast to the cheerful chaos of my own home. Each piece of furniture appeared to have been arranged by Charles with exactitude, and upon his desk his writing implements were laid out in ascending order of size.

Upon the highly polished surface, piles of neatly arranged papers were stacked and, moved by curiosity, I opened the desk drawer. Inside was a roll of letters tied up with a scarlet velvet ribbon. I placed my hand upon them, and my fingers hesitated for a moment, as if having a conscience of their own. Ignoring the warning, I pulled the ribbon undone, unfurled the letters and my eyes fell randomly upon the words written in Charles's hand:

My Dearest M
It is you whom I love . . . I know now that I cannot marry any other. . . .

My heart quickening, I read on:

It is unbearable torture without you . . . your intoxicating company, your violet-coloured eyes. . . .

Each word added to my growing rage:

If your father will look beyond my shortcomings, then I will ask him soon, I promise. . . .

This was too much to bear: to think that Charles had dared to number my own faults when he himself was acting with such deception! I hurled the letters across the room with fury.

'Mary, you deceitful and wicked wretch!'

And, taking the ink, I uncorked it and threw it across the collection of papers upon the desk. At that moment the door flew open and there stood Charles with the landlady, open-mouthed, at his side.

'Kate! What in heaven's name are you doing? How dare you interfere with my personal belongings?'

His face was contorted with a fierceness that I had never seen before, and the landlady hurried away down the stairs ready to share the gossip, Mr Wossal now being old news.

'Perhaps it is as well,' I said, harnessing courage and pointing to the letters scattered across the floor, 'as it seems that you and my sister have much to hide.'

Without saying a word, he strode purposefully across the room, grasped me behind the neck in a most ungentlemanly manner and threw me to my knees, roughly pushing my face close to the scatter of correspondence.

'Look who they are addressed to, Kate, can you see?'

I tried to focus my eyes urgently on what he was asking for, but I was bewildered with fear and shock at his behaviour.

'And what of the dates? Did you notice those?' he growled.

'Charles, you're hurting me!' But he was oblivious to it, seemingly driven by a need to exonerate himself. When he at last released me, he picked up the papers and began to read each one out loud.

'To Miss Maria Beadnell, Coniston Villa, Kent . . . dated the 2 February 1830.' He cast it angrily to the floor.

'And this one,' he continued, 'Miss Maria Beadnell . . . dated 25 June, 1830.' He threw that one to the floor too. One by one he read out the same name over and over, until he had cast each and every letter to the ground.

'Five years ago, Kate, five years! Your sister would have been little more than a child, and there is not even one mention of her name.'

'Then who was—? But I thought "Dearest M" must be . . .'

21

and I began to sob as I realized my foolishness.

'Kate, please don't cry,' Charles said with obvious discomfort, 'I hate it when a woman cries.'

'But who was she?'

Charles walked over to the window, took out his handkerchief and wiped away an unwelcome smudge on the glass. 'She was an unfortunate mistake, a changeable butterfly,' he sighed, 'and although she never intended to become my bride, she toyed with my emotions in the cruellest way that a woman can. She was the daughter of a wealthy banker and she was selfish, flirtatious and not at all suited to be the wife of a writer.'

'Then why did you keep those letters?' I asked querulously.

'Because, dear Kate,' he said with a wry smile, 'I am of a sentimental nature and prone, with the passing of time, to forget the reality of a situation. At the end of our friendship I asked Miss Beadnell, to return the letters that I sent her so that I might remind myself that I need a placid and steadfast love to become my wife.'

He walked back across the room, crouched down on his haunches and wiped away my tears with his handkerchief, 'And now I have found her.' He smiled.

I suddenly became aware of my appearance, my ink-stained hands and face, my red nose and my disarranged hair. I looked neither placid nor steadfast! Overcome with embarrassment, I begged Charles to forgive me and made him promise to speak of this to no one, especially Mary, whom I had so hastily accused.

'Yes, Kate, I promise, but you in turn must promise me something. You must promise me that you will always trust me, trust me unconditionally. I will not be questioned over my actions at any time, Kate, do you understand? Not at any time.'

His anger had frightened me and yet was I not to blame? Had I not provoked him? I made him the promise that he had requested and vowed that I would never be suspicious or doubt his morals again. But I did not know then that it would prove to be a promise impossible to keep.

CHAPTER THREE

October 1835
York Place, Chelsea

In October I fell ill. It was a month that I had always disliked, its fading crisped leaves and dusky afternoons, but now my melancholy was one of a physical nature. I was confined to my bed with a high fever and, as if to compound my low spirits, Charles was not free to visit me due to his growing work commitments. In his place he sent his sister, Fanny, a small, angular woman with plain features and a nose that looked as though it had been shaped by spending a good deal of time in other people's business.

Whenever I had asked Charles about meeting his parents he become strangely evasive and agitated as though it were a subject to be ashamed of. Fanny however, he had spoken of warmly, talking of happy childhood times spent together; but no matter how hard I looked, I could not find beneath her waspish personality the sister that Charles had spoken of so fondly. Taking off her coat and rolling up her sleeves as though she were about to perform an operation, Fanny set about plumping up my pillows and straightening my covers, with no thought that I might not want to be tossed about in such a ruthless manner. She had brought with her Charles's apologies and a basket of fruit.

'Are you sure he sent nothing else?' I asked, picking through the apples as if something more interesting might be hidden amongst them. 'Not even a note?'

'No, my dear,' she said coldly, 'what you see before you is a true reflection of his esteem for you.'

I was bitterly disappointed by his absence, his disagreeable sister and his dull gift.

Fanny's biting sarcasm did nothing to improve my ailing spirits. Not only did my heart sink at her daily visits, but I noticed that her main preoccupation seemed to be with how she might profit from the fortune of others. She took great delight in looking through my jewellery box, and would slip rings, necklaces and bracelets on and off with alarming sleight of hand. On one occasion, as she was leaving, I had cause to remind her, that she was still in possession of my grandmother's ruby ring, a silver brooch and my favourite hairpin.

' 'Tis only to be expected when my mind is quite taken up with caring for your every need!' she snapped.

Every day I enquired whether Charles had written me any word and her answer was always the same. 'He'll be too busy making his way in the world to find time for that, my dear.'

But what was most perplexing of all, was her delight at telling me of Charles's previous lovers when I had no desire to hear of them. One day when I had suffered an unrelenting headache, Fanny continued without letup. '. . . then there was Mary Ann Leigh, yes, when she was taken ill with the scarlet fever, he spent a whole afternoon choosing, "the softest gloves for the softest hands", I think was his turn of phrase.' She vigorously shook up my pillows again.

'Fanny, please, I don't feel well.'

'And then there was Maria Beadnell. . . .' My pulse quickened at the mention of her name. 'My! There was a romance for you. Nearly went out of his mind over that girl.'

'Fanny, I don't want to know about. . . .'

She sat me up and pushed a glass of water to my lips.

'The letters he sent that young woman . . . I doubt he'll ever really find a love like that again.'

My head throbbed.

Satisfied that her nursing duties had been fulfilled with the most tender care, she removed her pinafore saying, 'Well, I've got things to do, you mustn't keep me here talking all day. I'll call your sister to take over now and I'll be back again tomorrow, no doubt.'

I dropped back onto my pillows, trying to push Fanny's words from my mind. I did not want to think about Mary Ann Leigh or Maria, nor did I want to think about the reasons why Charles had not written, and seemed more concerned about his work than he was about me. Perhaps Fanny was right, maybe Charles could never love me as passionately as he had loved Maria. I thought about how often he had berated me whenever I voiced an opinion and began to wonder whether he was trying to mould me into a dull, agreeable puppet, someone who would not hinder his growing ambition.

Fanny closed the bedroom door behind her and I fell into a restless sleep: Charles was dressed in a sailor suit and stood beside a carriage which had the letter M monogrammed upon its door. Inside was seated a young woman, wearing a scarlet velvet ribbon in her dark hair. She extended her hand through the carriage window and Charles kissed it sadly. I stood upon the steps of Selwood Terrace watching them, and as the carriage pulled away, Charles turned to me, and in an instant his face changed to one of bitter disappointment.

With a pointed finger he ordered me into the house and then he began instructing me as to how to arrange the drawing room furniture. But wherever I placed a chair, he would move it elsewhere, wherever I hung a picture, he would shake his head disagreeably and take it down, and when I laid the table for dinner he set it all over again. With each opposing action that he performed, I became more restless and unsettled in my sleep.

When I protested at his unreasonable behaviour, he opened a large wooden chest and angrily ordered me into it. I pleaded with him that I would not fit, but he kept insisting until I obeyed. He brought down the lid upon me and padlocked it. The darkness was suffocating, but no matter how I struggled, the lid would not move and with a gasping breath I opened my eyes to find Mary's worried face hovering above me.

'I don't want to be trapped!' I cried out with a start.

'Catherine, dear Catherine,' she soothed, sponging my face and burning body, 'It's all right, I am here.'

'Mary,' I coughed, 'fetch me a pen...some paper.'

'Catherine, your fever will break soon, Please, stay calm.'

'No!' I insisted, 'I must write to him now, before I change my mind.'

I would not give in, and Mary, fearful at my feverish determination, ran and brought what I had asked for. She steadied my hand and I began to write:

Sir

I can no longer bear the absence of any word from you. If our engagement is not your dearest wish, then release me from it, and you will hear from me no more.

I signed it and pushed it into Mary's hand.

'You must see that Charles gets this immediately. Promise me, Mary.'

'Of course, dear Sister, only please, do not exert yourself any further. You must rest now.'

I nodded weakly and the darkness came again, but now it was a welcome darkness, a darkness no longer beset by dreams.

When the light returned, I raised a hand to shield the intrusive brightness from my eyes.

'Catherine, thank God!'

My mother, father and Mary, who had all being waiting anxiously at my bedside, moved to embrace me.

'We thought that we had lost you!' Mama wept hysterically.

Ignoring her dramatics I asked with urgency, 'But where is Charles? Did he come?'

Mary smiled her gentle smile and held out a bundle of letters and a small box. I pushed myself upright and took them from her with a frown.

'Open the gift, Catherine,' Papa said, stroking my hair.

'Is it from you, Papa?'

He shook his head, 'Open it and see.'

Inside the box was an exquisite antique bracelet, nestling in tissue paper. A small card resting on the top said simply: *I am yours alone, if you will still have me.*

Mary urged me to open the letters and I tore open the first which, according to the date, had been written over a fortnight ago, and began reading:

> *. . . so sorry that I cannot be with you . . . trying to make my way in the world....building a future for us. . . .*

Each letter, written in Charles's hand, assured me of his unchanging love, until finally I came to the last, which explained everything.

> *Fanny, it seems, for reasons best known to her, held back my letters from you. I hope that you will forgive her, as I have done, and be assured that a sisterly love for me was her only motive. I must finish the instalments I have committed myself to write and then I promise to be back at your side before the week is out.*
>
> *I remain ever yours,*
>
> *Charles*

CHAPTER FOUR

December 1835
York Place, Chelsea

December arrived, my health was restored and my spirits were lifted by the approaching festive season. I had planned to buy Charles a silver pen tray, but to my consternation, Mary had had the same idea. I petulantly pointed out that as Charles's intended the gift should be from me and, true to her nature, Mary agreed without opposition. Papa was to make Charles a present of an ivory-handled letter opener which had been his father's, and I thanked him saying that it would make a most handsome gift. But Mama, who was of an anxious nature, said she hoped that Charles would not cut himself on it.

'We'll no' want a groom wi' a missin' finger!' she warned in her Edinburgh lilt, with a shudder.

Papa stroked his sandy moustache, trying to hide a smile, and said, 'I have every confidence that the young man has a steady hand, my dear.'

On Christmas morning Mama hurried about, hastily straightening cushions and pushing clutter into overcrowded cupboards and under the sofa. 'I canna' see why we always ha' to make such a fuss when he visits us,' Mama complained. 'It's not as if we even know who the laddie's parents are.'

'Now, now, my love,' Papa counselled gently. 'Remember I too was once a struggling journalist with only my hopes and dreams for a wage. London has been good to me and I hope that it will look upon young Dickens as kindly.'

The ground and the rooftop were thick with snow and Charles arrived just before lunchtime shouting, 'Merry Christmas to the Hogarths!' We laughed as we realized that his hair had frozen to his scarf and while Mary led him to a fireside chair I fetched him a warm brandy. When I returned, he was deep in conversation with Papa.

'Do you know, sir, I spent most of the morning walking and thinking, and I never noticed the cold at all. Don't you find that this time of year makes you reflect on both the past and the future? And I found myself ruminating on an idea for a Christmas story. It was just a whisper of an idea, the beginning of something, something that I could not quite lay a hold of, but when it finally comes to me I shall capture it and put it down on paper for all to read.' He signed with frustration. 'But I am too caught up with *Sketches* at present to concentrate on anything else at all.'

Sketches by Boz was a collection of short stories that Charles had written over the last two years. They were now being put together in volume form, and he hoped that the money he earned from this might enable us to marry soon.

Papa stood up and patted him fondly on the shoulder. 'You keep at it, young man. If you carry on as you are, this will all just be the beginning for you, I am sure of it.'

Shaking off his momentary melancholy, Charles called us to his side saying, 'Hurry up everyone, I have presents for you all.'

Charles handed Papa a fine bottle of port, to Mama he gave some linen handkerchiefs and Georgina, a china doll. Only Mary and I were yet to open our gifts. Excitedly I unwrapped my own and took out a fringed shawl that was beautifully embroidered. I set it about my shoulders and glanced at Mama, who nodded and smiled with approval. I was just about to thank Charles, when Mary opened her gift and gasped as she took out of a small box a silver locket in the shape of a heart. I watched with dismay as Charles placed it around the neck of my sixteen-year-old sister who blushed and thanked him shyly.

There had to be some confusion: surely Charles had mixed up the gifts? Surely the heart-shaped locket must have been meant for me? My face flushed with the heat of my anger and I stared at the locket hanging at my sister's throat, longing to tear it from her. But a series of recollections stilled my hand. I recalled Charles's previous admonitions to mind my hasty temper. I thought again about his disapproval when I had been short with Mary on our visit to the theatre and lastly I remembered the embarrassing scene that I had caused over Maria Beadnell. So what did I do? I swallowed my resentment and said nothing. And here was a beginning: the first of many times that I would suppress my own feelings in search of Charles's approval. But wasn't this the role of a good and loyal wife, the yielding of her own will and opinion?

That evening, I said to Mary what could never be said to Charles.

She had not removed the locket from around her neck and even now, as she lay in bed, she caressed it gently between her finger and thumb, deep in thought.

My voice broke into her reverie. 'Mary, if I were ever to consider giving Charles up, could you see yourself in my place? As his love, I mean?' I tried to mask the bitter note of jealousy that my voice betrayed.

Mary sat up in bed abruptly.

'Catherine, whatever are you implying? How could you say such a thing? Charles is yours and yours alone. It is true that I had a girlish fancy for him once, but I can only think of him now as a much-loved brother, and nothing more.'

'Are you sure, Mary? Are you sure that you have not unknowingly encouraged any intentions he may have towards you?'

'Catherine, you don't know your own sister if you could entertain such thoughts. How can you doubt Charles's love for you? Remember the beautiful bracelet he sent you, and his letters of devotion?'

I knew that her words were true, and I began to wonder if there was something wrong with me. How could I doubt Mary's loyalty and integrity? But of Charles I was still not sure.

Over the holiday, I watched him closely as he seemed ever more drawn to Mary's side, laughing at her jokes, complimenting her on her musical accomplishments, bombarding her with ideas for stories that he vowed he would one day put down on paper. When the New Year arrived Charles told me that he had decided to leave Selwood Terrace and return to Furnival's Inn as it was closer to his work in the City. My heart sank at the thought of starting our married life in those dull grey lodgings, but what he said next drained the colour from my face.

'Kate, I have been thinking – it is selfish of me to take you further away from your family as you will be spending a good deal of time on your own once we are wed. Perhaps it would be good for Mary to come and live with us at Furnival's Inn so that she can keep you company.'

A feeling of panic flooded through my veins; I could see the silver locket twirling before my eyes, once again I saw Charles fasten it tenderly around Mary's neck; lastly I saw the look of adoration in his eyes.

'Charles, I do not—'

He lifted his hand. 'No, Kate, you do not have to thank me. I shall not change my mind. In fact, Mary has already agreed to it.'

It was nothing unusual, I knew. Many young sisters lived with an older sibling until their own wedding day, but I did not want it. I did not want it at all. I feared that Mary would continue to outshine me under my very own roof; however, what Charles had decided I could only concede to. But how could he know that it was his ambiguous feelings about Mary that continued to lie at the heart of all my insecurities?

CHAPTER FIVE

2 April 1836
St Lukes's Church, Chelsea

The day of the wedding arrived. I had not been able to eat one mouthful of the kippers and poached eggs that Alice had put before me that morning, and no amount of cajoling on her part could induce an appetite in me.

'Well don't come a-blamin' me, lassie, if ye faint away in the middle of the vows!' Alice scowled, taking the plate away.

I sat at my dressing table struggling with trembling fingers and thumbs to pin a piece of heather onto my dress. Mama had given it to me for good luck, but it stubbornly refused to be fixed as if withholding its blessing on my future happiness. It is naturally every young woman's dream to reach this day in her life, yet I wondered, is it possible? Can one person really make another happy for a whole lifetime?

I thought about my parents' marriage. It had been twenty-one years since they wed in their native Scotland, both of them barely twenty years old. Papa had grown steady and wise, with a good head for business, and Mama, well, Mama was not steady or wise at all, but Papa loved her nonetheless and indulged her histrionics. So perhaps there was no perfect pairing. Perhaps the most that one could hope for was a mutual acceptance of one another's shortcomings.

And what of the shortcomings of my own intended? I loved

him deeply, so would that not cover 'a multitude of sins'? I hesitated to answer, realizing how little I truly knew him, his fears, his secrets. I wondered what lay hidden in that dark place, the secret person of the heart that no one really knows, except God and ourselves? True, I had witnessed his ambition for success, but hard work is not a vice, is it? And I had also been on the receiving end of his temper. But should a man not show righteous indignation when his integrity is questioned? Had I not unduly provoked him? I reassured myself that this was true and that I should give him absolutely no cause to be angry with me once we were wed.

Yesterday, Mama had spoken to me late into the evening, advising me of a wife's responsibilities and how I should never permit Charles to be concerned about domestic matters.

'Ye must allow him to concentrate entirely on his work, m'dearie. Your haime should be a place of peace and refuge for him.'

Fine words coming from Mama! But true even so. However, I feared that I too should somehow be inadequate; I had never run a house before and I was not in the least organized by nature. I sighed wearily, and addressed my reflection in the dressing-table mirror.

'Come now, Catherine, these sober thoughts are subduing all the romantic fancies that should accompany such a day. No more of this gloomy mood, do you hear? This is your wedding day, after all.'

There was a gentle tap on the door which brought me to my senses.

'Are you quite well, my dear?'

'Yes, of course, Papa,' I called hastily. 'I was just coming.' I attempted to secure my corsage once more and, at last, I succeeded.

'There!' I smiled to myself. 'You see, everything will be just fine.'

Papa had spared no expense in arranging the wedding of his eldest daughter. I had chosen cousin Elizabeth, Mary, and little

33

Georgina to be my bridesmaids, and when Papa saw us together, he pronounced himself to be 'the proudest man in all England'.

We stepped out onto the pavement of York Place to find that the day was sunny but breezy, and I feared that the wind might tug at my bonnet and snatch it away completely, but Mary, with her calming touch, came to my aid with a pin to secure both my hat and my confidence.

I grasped at her wrist, 'Mary, I—'

She put a finger to my lips. 'Catherine, it is far too late to give way to doubts now. Marry him and determine to be happy.' And she and Papa assisted me up into the waiting carriage.

As Papa walked me down the aisle, I watched Charles's face intently to see whether his eyes wavered to Mary, following behind me radiant with the bloom of youth. But his eyes never left mine for a moment and after saying my vows all my anxieties faded away.

'Dear, sweet, clumsy Kate, at last we are wed,' he whispered in my ear. The vicar proclaimed that he may kiss the bride, and I blushed as the congregation rang with applause.

The wedding breakfast held at York Place was an array of temptation: cooked hams, lobster salad and game pie laid out alongside champagne, trifles, blancmange and fruit jellies. After I had thought that I could smile and shake hands no more, I noticed a portly, ruby-cheeked man who was helping himself to a rather large portion of game pie. He whistled chirpily, as if he had not seen a spread like this in a good while, and then put a leg of chicken in each of his pockets for good measure.

Charles's face went pale at the sight of him, and then blood-red. 'What the blazes is he doing here? That man will be the undoing of me!' He excused himself from my side and, with a purposeful stride, crossed the room to where the fellow was now wrapping another portion of pie in his oversized handkerchief. My eyes grew wide as I watched while Charles remonstrated with him, and the man, looking sheepish, took the offending items from his pockets and handed them back to Charles. I could not hear what was being said but my husband behaved in the manner of a disappointed father scolding his child. The man, thoroughly shamed, nodded apologetically at each admonition, and after giving one last emphatic nod, he meekly followed Charles to my side.

In a moment, he had regained his buoyancy, wiped his greasy fingers on his waistcoat and held out his hand in greeting.

'John Dickens, ma'am,' he enthused, 'pleased to make your h'acquaintance at last.'

His clothes looked as though they had seen the inside of a pawnbroker's shop on more than a few occasions and I turned to Charles for an explanation.

'My father.' Charles coughed with embarrassment.

'Oh, I see,' I said, taking the greasy hand as graciously as I could manage. 'And your dear wife, sir, is she here too?' which was the only thing that I could think to say, feeling quite perplexed by the situation.

Standing with Fanny was a slightly built woman with sharp features, who, I was alarmed to note, picked up the wedding gifts one by one from the table and examined each one with a squinted eye.

'That's my Lizzie, over there,' said Mr Dickens proudly, and when he called his spouse she jumped, as if being caught red-handed in some shady act.

She joined her oily husband's side and exclaimed joyfully, 'Fancy! My Charles marrying the daughter of a gentleman! Who would have believed it?' and she rubbed her hands together in a most gleeful manner. Charles quickly dispatched his errant parents to a table in a distant corner of the garden with a hissed warning that they should touch nothing, and that under no circumstance should his mother dance.

When it was time to leave for our honeymoon, it was hard to say goodbye to my family and to the life that I had known before.

'Look at her, George,' my mother sniffed. 'Our wee lassie, all grown up and now a wife.'

While Papa embraced me, Mr Dickens chanced to

congratulate his son and whispered discreetly in Charles's ear. Charles rolled his eyes skywards, sighed wearily and took out a coin from his pocket which he deposited in his father's ready hand.

Mr Dickens tipped his hat in appreciation. 'Lord, bless you, Charlie. I knew you wouldn't refuse your old pa. Not now you're a-makin' your way in the world.'

We stepped into the waiting carriage to set off for the village of Chalk where we planned to spend a week in a small cottage.

Here, at last, we could lose ourselves in each other's company without distraction, interruption or thoughts of anyone else and, apart from brief moments when Charles would slip away to that distant place in his mind – a place where not even I could reach him – he gave me his undivided attention and said that he could never have imagined that he would find such contentment in his life.

CHAPTER SIX

Summer 1836
Furnival's Inn, London

In the weeks and months that followed our wedding, *The Pickwick Papers* became an unexpected success and I was having to share Charles with his editor, his illustrator, his publishers and a growing number of admiring readers. He had been right about my need for Mary's companionship; there were days when the hours seemed to be filled with nothing more than the ticking of the clock and waiting for him to return home.

Even then, he often worked late into the night and I would wake in the early hours to see that his place in bed beside me was still empty. If I went into the sitting room, I would find him writing in the guttering light of a candle. Or, sometimes, he would simply be slumped across his work asleep, the pen still between his finger and thumb. I never woke him, for when I did he would not return to bed, but would take up his pen again with great haste, distressed by his somnolence.

If today he had produced twenty pages, then tomorrow it must be five more, and he would labour on and on with unflagging resolve until he had reached his goal.

'After all, Kate,' he would say with great earnestness, 'my luck could change in a moment.'

But his success brought with it jealousy and resentment from some of his former associates. An editor named John Macrone, with whom Charles had previously worked, was now calling upon him to produce a novel that Charles had once discussed writing, but as this had only been a verbal agreement, Charles did not feel bound to keep it. Macrone was unreasonable and threatened legal action if he was not compensated for his loss and, with no apparent head for business, Charles found himself handing over the copyright to some of his earlier work, and the loss was now his own.

That evening he came home in the foulest of tempers. Mary and I sat reading in what remained of the evening light. We heard the door to the lodgings slam, and Charles ascended the stairs to our rooms cursing to himself. My body tensed in anxious anticipation.

'If I could get hold of that opportunist by the throat, I would squeeze it and shake him until there was not a breath left in his body!'

He hurled his hat onto the sofa, walked across to the dining table and struck it violently with his cane. 'Never again shall I let anyone force my hand! Never! How dare he?'

I felt quite frightened by his vehemence and was at a loss as to what to say or do; to me, Charles's moods were like a foreign language that I could neither read nor understand. Mary, on the other hand, interpreted every twitch of his physiognomy with the ease of a native speaker. With her usual perception she whispered that she would fetch him a glass of brandy and I got up and tentatively went to his side.

I placed my hand gently on his arm. 'Come, my love, whatever has taken place, surely all that matters is you and I, and our love for one another. Have you forgotten that?' I smiled nervously.

He looked at my hand and then at me, as though I had quite taken leave of my senses.

'Kate, can you not conceive that my world now reaches far beyond these insignificant walls?'

His voice was full of contempt and, for a moment, I wondered if he was joking.

'Charles?'

He shook off my hand abruptly. 'You have no idea of my life and what I do each day, do you? No idea at all.'

Mary came back into the room and almost collided with me as I fled through the door in distress.

'Catherine? Catherine!'

But I did not answer. I ran down the stairs and taking the shawl that hung on a hook by the door, I hurried out into the courtyard and pushed past a small group of loiterers who looked on with idle interest. Mary called after me from the doorway, but all that I could hear were the words that Charles had spoken: 'My world reaches far beyond these insignificant walls!'

I ran across the market square, which was now empty save for the rats that crawled in the shadows and sniffed at rotten fruit. Fuelled by my anger I walked on aimlessly from one place to another, ruminating over my husband's thoughtless words which tumbled around in my head. I supposed that he might be worrying a little over me now. Well, it would do him good to worry about me for a change, instead of his writing.

The sound of raucous laughter spilled out onto the streets from the coaching inns. A lamplighter eyed me with suspicion and raised his shabby brown hat.

' 'Tis late to be out, miss. Are you all right there?'

I nodded, saying that I hadn't realized the time and that I was just on my way back home to Furnival's Inn.

'You'll want to be a-turnin' around then miss,' he grinned, 'you're headin' the wrong way.' His teeth were quite brown and rotten and, although he meant no harm at all, I felt that I was being sized up for a meal by a hungry fox. I pulled my shawl tightly about me, turned around and hurried away.

The streets that bustled with life during the day had become strangely unfamiliar now that it was dark. My anger dissolved into a feeling of panic as I realized that I was completely lost. My shawl flapped about me in the wind, I heard soft footsteps in the shadows, and turned to look over my shoulder. A figure darted back into the shadows and I began to quicken my pace. I passed under a bridge and swallowed hard, my heart hammering within my chest.

On the opposite side of the street, a red-haired woman stumbled and laughed, clinging on to the arm of a gentleman soldier. I hurried across the road to beg for their aid. 'You must help me. Please! I think that someone is following me.'

The woman laughed again and pushed me away. Her companion raised his cane. 'Be off with you! Can't you see that we're busy?'

I heard the footsteps of my pursuer again and I began to run. But as I came to the end of the street, my escape was blocked by a dead end. I turned, and in that moment in the flickering gaslight I saw him. His face was partly obscured by a tangle of dark hair through which his eyes blazed with violent intent. He grabbed me around the neck snarling, 'Your jewellery, I want it!'

He tightened his grip on my throat and in a moment of clarity, I pulled off my rings and hurled them as far as I could down the alleyway. He threw me to the floor and he stumbled after them fearful that they would be lost in the mud. He did not return and I lay curled up on the ground, still and shaken with the horror of what had happened. Time passed.

The outline of a tattered boot came into focus and I sat up with shock at the sight of it.

'You 'urt, miss?'

A young woman, her hands thrust deep into the pockets of her striped skirt, chewed at the pipe in her mouth, and looked down at me with curiosity.

Without a word of answer I took to my feet and began to run as far as my breath would allow until I saw the spire of St. Etheldreda's Church, pointing the way home, a signpost in the moon's light. It was such a welcome vision that I nearly cried at the sight of it and I kept my eyes firmly fixed upon it until I passed back through the market and at last turned into the courtyard of Furnival's Inn.

In the hazy light of the street lamps I could see Charles and

Mary standing in the doorway. Mary was crying on his shoulder and, as I drew closer, I could hear her anguished voice. 'Where can she have got to? We have looked everywhere, Charles.'

My husband raised his eyes, saw me and blinked for a moment, not at all sure if I was real.

'My God, Kate, where in heaven's name have you been?'

His voice betrayed both anger and relief. But, as I came toward him, his face turned pale at the sight of my bruised and bloodied neck.

'Dear Lord, what has happened?' he whispered fearfully.

There were many tears shed as later, wrapped in a blanket and sitting by the fire, I related my awful ordeal.

'Kate, I must insist,' Charles began sternly and then catching Mary's eye, softened his tone, 'What I mean to say is that you must promise me, that you will never do anything so foolish again.'

I nodded and dropped my head against his shoulder with a sob.

A few days later, at Charles's suggestion, we returned to the cottage in Chalk. It was just what I needed to soothe my troubled nerves. The small latticed windows opened out onto the surrounding countryside and, while Charles worked away diligently, safe in the knowledge that he would not be disturbed by any more nocturnal wandering on my part, I lay in bed, hypnotized by the sunlight resting upon his dark curly hair. Every so often he would stop writing and catch me watching him with contentment. The encounter with the thief had been a terrible shock and yet my misfortune had brought with it an unexpected blessing: some time with my husband. At that moment I felt a sense of peace that I realized had been missing ever since our last visit here.

When we returned home, sadly the weather changed. The wind and rain drove hard across the courtyard dampening everything with its persistence. Large pools of water had formed on the ground and our lodgings looked more uninviting than ever. I peered intently at the faces of the men hanging about our doorway. Was *he* here . . . hidden among them . . . waiting for me? I looked at their large, dirty hands and their twitching fingers, and instinctively raised a protective hand to my throat. Stepping across the threshold, I shuddered, imagining that I could feel his breath once more on my face, and I did not dare to look in a mirror for fear that I might see the reflection of his face.

The heavy atmosphere outside somehow seeped through the walls of Furnival's Inn and suddenly it seemed that Charles and I had very little to say to one another. My eyes fell upon the dent in the dining table where he had struck it with his cane and I realized that in the chaos of my disappearance, the preceding discord between us had been forgotten. Charles had still not apologized for his unkind words and I inwardly acknowledged that the trip to Chalk had been a reparation, a means of making amends on his part. But beyond this, I knew that my husband would never admit that he had done anything wrong.

CHAPTER SEVEN

November 1836
Furnival's Inn, London

October came and went, and I felt my usual melancholy at the onset of winter. Charles often chastised me for burning the oil in almost every room, but I loathed the dreary days and long evenings exacerbated by these grey lodgings that I could never think of as my home. Thoughts about the previous occupants flitted across my mind. I wondered, had these rooms ever meant anything to *them*? Somebody had once cared enough to decorate the walls in the paper that was now faded and curling at the edges; and the portraits that were placed about the room, someone had cared enough to arrange them so.

The faces that smiled back from those gilt frames were strangers to me and I was sure that they had smiled just as cheerfully in the pawnbroker's shop window, from where they had no doubt come. They appeared to possess a sense of happiness and dignity that I had not felt since my life at York Place. I missed Mama and Papa, I missed Alice, our Scottish servant and I missed my little Georgina who had filled our house with life. If only I had some useful purpose, then maybe I would feel more settled here. Charles had made it clear that my role was to see to the running of the home and nothing more, but he was hardly ever here to see that I was trying hard in this endeavour.

Even now, I could not put a name to the fanciful duties that I had envisioned for myself before our wedding. Perhaps it had been to apply balm to the wounds inflicted upon my husband by his working life. Or, maybe, it had been simply to offer companionship by the fireside when he arrived home. However, it was Mary about whom he fretfully enquired as soon as he stepped over the threshold of Furnival's Inn, and it was Mary who provided the balm with her soothing tone at the end of a trying day.

Outside, I heard laughter coming from the courtyard below and it drew me to the window. The view from here was usually uninspiring; our rooms were on the back of the building and the only variation in scenery came from the shifting patterns of the sunlight across the neglected courtyard. If I had had a clear view down Leather Lane or Brooke Street, I would have only seen the projecting upper storeys and wooden beams of lodging houses more dismal that my own. But today, as I looked down, I saw Charles and Mary carrying a small ornamental table between the two of them and laughing as they struggled to walk in time together without dropping it.

'Move a little more this way, Mary,' Charles coaxed.

'My arms are aching! You said it wasn't far,' she giggled.

'Well, let us put it down for a moment then,' Charles replied, good-naturedly.

The scene did nothing to lift my mood; I had had an attack of nerves that morning, which was becoming quite common since the theft of my jewellery, and I had declined the opportunity to venture out. I was now expecting our first child and I resented the carefree attitude of my sister and my husband.

'What on earth are you doing?' I called down from the window.

Mary smiled up at me, her face glowing. 'Don't be vexed, Catherine. We have brought a surprise for you. Look, a pretty table to put at your bedside.'

'Couldn't you have had it delivered?' I said, with irritation.

'Why tip the delivery boy for doing what I could manage

myself?' Charles called cheerfully. 'I have carried it most of the way. Mary has only assisted me for the last hundred yards.'

He spoke partly with the pleasure of having saved an unnecessary expense. He was not a mercenary man by any means, but I had begun to notice that an excessive fear of debt seemed always to accompany him, and any expenditure must first be justified as absolutely necessary in his mind before any financial outlay, no matter how small. He spoke also with the realization that perhaps it had not been at all seemly to allow a young lady to struggle alongside him in such an undignified manner.

Later, over lunch, I was quiet and withdrawn and I did not join in the light-hearted conversation that flowed backwards and forwards across the table.

'. . . what do you say, Kate? Kate?'

Charles put down his knife and fork and sighed. 'For goodness' sake, Kate, what on earth is wrong with you today? You refused to come out to the town this morning, you will not join us in conversation over lunch and you have not even thanked Mary and I for the gift that we bought you. Don't you like the little table?'

I stared with indifference at my untouched meal. 'What use is a table, if the house that I am to place it in is detestable to me? How can I bring a child into the world and feel any joy at the prospect of bringing it up here? There is nothing in these rooms that belongs to me; the furniture is not ours, the rugs are not ours; the portraits on the walls are not even of our relatives. Nothing here is mine. Nothing at all.'

There was no passion in my voice, no vital energy whatsoever.

'But it will not always be this way, my love,' Charles said with encouragement. 'You know that I mean for us to have something better, but you must be patient. I cannot work any harder, you know that, and you must not make me feel that what I am doing at present is not good enough. That is very mean-spirited of you.'

He began cutting away vigorously at his meat, which was a

little coarse, and in exasperation he dropped his knife and fork with a clatter. 'Oh, bother! Kate, why must you always choose the cheapest cuts? We are not paupers, you know.'

I was just about to remind him how frequently he prompted me to be more careful with the housekeeping when Mary, sensing disquiet, calmly intervened.

'Perhaps if we had a dinner party and invited all the family and some of your friends, Charles. Some of your new colleagues, people that Catherine and I have not yet met. That would surely lift Catherine's spirits.'

She turned to me for confimation, but before I could reply, Charles jumped at the idea. 'Yes! Of course. What a capital suggestion.' He wiped his mouth with a napkin, threw it down on the table and immediately got up and began to pace the room.

'Let me see. We shall have good food.' He eyed me with a marked look, 'Wine, music – your father could play his cello for us, and we could have some dancing. What do you think, eh, Kate?'

'It seems that between the two of you, it has been decided.' I replied with an air of weary resignation.

The following week, our rooms at Furnival's Inn were lit up with extra candles. I had to admit that all in all it did look rather inviting, and my spirits lifted a little. Charles inspected the table setting several times, straightening the knives and forks, refolding the napkins, giving the wine glasses a final polish until he was completely satisfied.

'Now, what about the seating arrangements?'

It was a rhetorical question rather than an invitation for an opinion from me.

'Your parents can sit here at the top, next to you and me, Kate; my sister, Fanny, and her new husband, Albert, next to them; William and Isabella Thackeray there, and cousin Elizabeth and Mary, with Daniel Maclise and my brother Fred opposite them. Yes, I think that will do it. Or . . . should I put. . . ?' I left him to his vacillations.

Mama and Papa were the first to arrive, followed by Fanny

and Albert. Mama took off her cloak and then peered at my face. Not at all satisfied with what she saw, she began to fuss around me.

'Ye look a little pale, m'dearie. Are ye sure that ye are up to having too much excitement this evening? Ye've not been yourself at all since that awful incident.'

'Well, if she will go running out into the streets in the dead of night, what can she expect?' Fanny interjected, never one to miss a chance to reprove me.

Charles quickly interposed. 'George – Mrs Hogarth, how good of you both to come. Please, let me introduce you to a dear colleague of mine, a fellow author and fine illustrator I might add: Mr William Thackeray.'

The tall, curly-haired man with a genial face smiled and shook hands in turn with my parents. 'Pleased to meet you, sir, madam.'

'And this is his wife, Isabella.'

She was a rounded, pleasant-faced woman, who had no remarkable features to speak of other than her thick dark hair, which was looped in plaits on either side of her head.

Fred Dickens arrived not far behind another of Charles's new friends, the artist Daniel Maclise. I had only met Fred once before and had immediately warmed to him. He was near to my own age and still had a good deal of boyish mischief in his eyes. Within a few moments of his arrival, he had elicited good-natured laughter between himself, Cousin Elizabeth and Mary.

Mr Maclise, who was very handsome and originated from Ireland, took off his hat and held out his hand to greet me. 'Madam, I am happy to make your acquaintance at last.' He put his hand inside his coat pocket and pulled out a small package which he placed in my hand. 'For you, madam, although I am only the means of bringing it to you. The gift itself is from your husband,' he explained.

Intrigued, I unwrapped it with great haste and inside found a framed miniature of Charles.

'Mr Maclise!' I laughed with delight. 'You have captured his likeness exactly.'

'Do you like it, Kate?' Charles asked.

I was touched by his thoughtfulness. 'Yes,' I whispered, quite overcome for a moment. 'Yes, it is wonderful'

'You can put me up there.' He grinned, gesturing to the wall. 'In among the gallery of unknowns.'

'Oh no, not at all, my love,' I protested. 'I will hang it at my bedside, above the little table that you bought for me.'

Daniel Maclise nodded in agreement. 'I do not think that you will ever sit in a gallery of unknowns, Mr Dickens. And I think you'll find that this is not the last commission that I'll be given to paint your likeness.'

The meal, to my complete relief, was a success. The meat had been bought, on Mama's recommendation, from her butcher in Fulham and it was the most tender side of beef that I had ever tasted. There were noises of appreciation throughout all the courses and Charles caught my eye with a wink and a smile. A realization of joy flooded through my body. At last! This was what I had been looking for: the incomparable feeling of having the approval of one's husband.

After our dessert, we pushed back the table and arranged the chairs in a circle so that we could hear Fanny sing. Albert fussed around her devotedly, but could not please her no matter how he adjusted the music stand; and when he was unable to turn over the pages of her music without fumbling, I felt painfully sorry for the poor fellow and wished that the ground would open up and save him from his humiliation and Fanny's withering glare. Papa followed with a round of merry tunes on his cello and Charles danced with enthusiasm, swinging me around without a care for my being with child. Fred excitedly mimicked his brother, confident that whatever Charles could do, he could do equally well. He divided himself more than fairly between Mary and Elizabeth and even managed to persuade Mama to dance with him, despite her protestations of a weak heart! Between them Mr Maclise and Papa happily shared the contents of the whisky decanter, and if Papa's playing suffered any for it, we did not notice.

In the early hours of the morning we bid our guests goodbye amid much suppressed laughter and reprimands of 'Shhhh!' from Fanny. Charles stood in the courtyard and waved them off energetically, still full of boundless energy. It had been a wonderful evening. I was happy, and what mattered more than anything else in the world was that I had managed to be a success in the eyes of my husband. I turned to Mary to thank her for suggesting such a wonderful evening, but, unexpectedly, Mary was not at my side. When I trod quietly back up the stairs to the sitting room, I found her fanning herself with an unsteady hand and looking quite pale. I knelt down at her side and took her hand.

'Dear Mary, whatever is the matter?'

She smiled, with greater concern for me than for herself and said, 'It is nothing to worry about, dearest. Young Frederick quite wore me out with his jokes and vigorous dancing, that is all.'

'Still, you do not look well, Sister. Let me help you to your room.' I took her arm and, despite her reassurances of good health, I noticed that she trembled slightly and leaned upon me rather heavily. How selfish I was. I had been so caught up in my own dejection, that I had not given any thought to the adjustments that Mary had had to make. She, too, had left behind the comfort and familiarity of York Place, the support of Mama and Papa and the help of a housemaid, and yet, her only concern had been to cement the happiness of Charles and myself. I had overburdened her, I was sure of it. I suddenly realized all that Mary had done for Charles and me and how her presence in my home, rather than being a hindrance to my marriage, as I had once feared, had in fact eased the relationship along.

Full of remorse, I kissed her goodnight. Her face was damp with perspiration and at that moment I was chilled by the most terrible thought: what would become of my marriage without her?

'Mary?' I whispered, gripped with horror and fear. 'You won't ever leave me, will you?'

CHAPTER EIGHT

January 1837
Furnival's Inn, London

'Yes, it is true, the wife of a writer needs the patience of a saint!' Isabella laughed.

With the growth of Charles's fame in the City, there was an increase in the number of visitors who called at our door. Some came merely out of curiosity to see where the 'Inimitable Boz' was living out his life. Others formed part of our close circle of friends – among these was Isabella Thackeray. Since our first meeting she and I had quickly found that there was much that we had in common and she had become a regular visitor to our home. When I described how Charles would work late into the night and then grunt with irritation the following morning, she would nod and laugh with understanding. It was such a blessing to have someone who could comprehend what I had thought to be my unique position.

Isabella had been born the eldest of twelve children and long before she became a mother herself, she had wiped sticky hands and faces, calmed boisterous siblings and spoon-fed fidgety babies. She was a neat-handed seamstress, a competent cook and, if she had not been the most kind-hearted friend that a woman could wish for, I should have been envious of her talents. Instead I counted myself lucky to have found her companionship.

Her benevolence also extended to those whom others would not have welcomed so freely. She had befriended a widowed Jewess, old Mrs Rozawich, and her daughter Esther, and occasionally they would accompany Isabella on her visits to Furnival's Inn. Old Mrs Rozawich did not smile a great deal and her lips were permanently set in a thin line of animosity. But I supposed that it was hardly surprising. Despite the presentation of the Bill of Emancipation, the Jews were still viewed with suspicion and prejudice by many. Isabella, however, looked beyond these things and saw only another human being in need of charity. I was sure that beneath her hostile exterior, Mrs Rozawich was touched by Isabella's kindness, but having been rejected and moved along so often in her life, her trust and thanks were not easily won. Her husband, Saul, had been dead for fifteen years. He had left Russia with few belongings and it was the money which their son, Peter, earned from his second-hand plate and jewellery stall, that kept Esther and her mother with a home to call their own.

Esther was unmarried, and whenever she visited she had the curious habit of scrutinizing me over her spectacles, as though she were trying to fathom out what it was that had qualified me to achieve what she had not: namely, entrance into the holy estate of matrimony. I could almost hear her thinking, 'How could such an unremarkable woman have married a man like Mr Dickens?'

'Perhaps he thought that her father had money,' I overheard Mrs Rozawich whisper in explanation to her daughter, as they were leaving one day.

On 6 January, 1837 my first child, Charles Culliford Dickens, was born. Yet despite his being the sweetest child that a mother could wish for, I could not seem to feel close to him and the walls of Furnival's Inn pressed in on me more than ever. Mary and Mama were my constant companions and I do not think that I would have survived my confinement without them. It seemed as though I was blessed with neither physical nor emotional strength.

One evening, a few weeks after the arrival of baby Charles, my husband came home earlier than expected. He bounded up the stairs calling me with great excitement in his voice.

'Kate! Kate! Where are you? I have some good news for you.'

Charles opened the bedroom door and, seeing Mama, his expression changed.

'Oh, Mrs Hogarth. I didn't think that you would still be here.'

'Well is this no' a mother's place, to be with her daughter at such a time?'

'Yes, of course. I thank you kindly.' He bowed his head in a polite gesture which belied his wish that she leave immediately. 'But I have something that I would like to speak to Kate about.'

'Well don't mind me. Go ahead, laddie, go ahead.'

Charles cleared his throat. 'I meant for us to be alone, ma'am.'

Mama took umbrage at this and immediately began gathering her things to leave.

'Well! Never let it be said that I outstay m'welcome!'

'Please. Mrs Hogarth, I didn't mean—'

But Mama was not to be placated and left with the words, 'I shall no' come again until *Catherine* invites me.'

Charles was not unduly worried by the thought that he might not see Mama again for a while. He did not possess the same spirit of calmness and patience that Papa had, and found that too much time spent in Mama's company made him irritable. He sat down on the bed at my side and took my hand.

'Kate, I am sorry if I upset your mama, but I have some wonderful news for you: I think that I have found a new home for us.'

This certainly was good news and I forgot all about my dejection and sat upright in bed.

'Listen to this, Kate. It is near to the parks and theatres that you so enjoy, and it is in a private road with a porter at the gate, so we will have no more busybodies enquiring at our door. And as for its size, it has twelve rooms over four floors.'

He laughed with excitement and clasped my hand tighter.

'Did you hear that? Twelve rooms!'

'Charles, slow down, I cannot take in all that you are saying.' I did not yet dare to hope that what he was telling me was true. 'Are you sure that we will be able to afford such a place?'

Disappointed at my lukewarm response, his countenance fell for a moment. 'Do you not want to move, Kate? I thought that you were unhappy here. I thought that that was what you wanted.'

'Of course I want to move, my love, but I know how you worry about money, and I just want to be sure that my happiness will not be at the expense of your own.'

'Then if that is your only concern, worry no more. I have received an advance from the publishers on my next novel and it will more than cover the rent. I have taken the lease for six months, and if we are happy there then I shall extend it.'

So it was really true. At last we would be leaving this place and moving to our own home.

'There is much to be done, Kate, furniture to buy, staff to employ. How do you feel about having a cook and a maid?'

'But, Charles—'

He raised his hand to quiet my doubts. 'A cook and a maid I said we need and a cook and a maid it shall be.'

He reached into his waistcoat pocket and took out a crumpled piece of paper. He smoothed it out and began reading:

Wanted – A cook who will not be wasteful. Early riser, clean habits and discreet nature. 5s. per week for the most suitable applicant.
Apply: Mr Charles Dickens, Furnival's Inn, Holborn.

He looked up, explaining, 'I have placed it in *The Times* this morning.

I nodded with approval. 'It is very good, Charles.'

'As for a maid, I think for now she will have to be a maid-of-all-work and then perhaps in time we can find a scullery maid to help out too.'

Our own maid. I could hardly believe it – and a cook too! I would need some advice, I knew that, and I immediately thought of Mama.

'Mary, will be delighted when she hears of this,' I enthused.

Charles coloured a little and said with a cough, 'I think you will find that Mary already knows. You see, I took her with me to see the house.' His voice quickened a little in hasty explanation. 'You have not been well, Kate, and have not felt like venturing out, so, of course, I knew that you could not come with me.'

I tried to hide my disappointment behind a gracious nod. 'I see. Then I'm sure that if Mary likes it, it will be fine for me too.'

Among the responses to Charles's advertisement was one from a cook who had worked for a clergyman. Her letter explained that her former employer had had only a small parish and, consequently, they had learned to live frugally. Charles had not wanted to interview her at Furnival's Inn, so he arranged a meeting at York Place where Mama would also help me to choose a maid.

Mrs Knapman arrived at three o' clock prompt and, as Charles could not abide lateness, this immediately went in her favour. She waited in the sitting room, while Charles momentarily paced backward and forward in the hallway rehearsing a few questions. When he entered the room with a confident greeting, and began to outline his wishes, no one would have believed that he was a young man of twenty-five who had never before employed a servant.

'I am sure you appreciate, Mrs Knapman, that I am becoming very well known in the City and will have all sorts of enquiries into my business when you are out and about. But you understand exactly what will be required of you, I hope?'

'Yes, Mr Dickens, you can rely on me, sir – discretion will be my watch word. And I can reassure you that I will not be wasteful; in my last position I learned to cook on a budget. "Waste not, want not", was the motto of my previous master, sir, and I have learned to live by it. Yes I have.'

And that is how Mrs Knapman came to be our cook. As for a maid, Mama's butcher recommended his niece from Yorkshire. She was aged just sixteen and looking for her first position. Mama had thought that as she was younger than me, I would not feel awkward giving her instruction and that I could train her up to suit Charles and myself. With Mama's help I drew up a list of duties.

I was pleased to see that Mary Williams was a strong-looking girl who looked as though she would handle her work in a capable manner. She arrived with her mother and listened carefully as I outlined the list of tasks. She nodded and said very quietly, 'Yes, madam, I can do all of those things.'

'Well then, I am happy with your uncle's recommendation and will write to let you know when we shall require you to start.'

As a final point, Mama suggested that Mary change her name to Emily so that there would not be any confusion with our own Mary and, as neither Mary nor her mother seemed perturbed by it, Emily she became.

In the weeks that followed, we began to make arrangements to move into 48 Doughty Street. While Georgina circled the room and rocked the baby in her arms, Mary began packing up our clothing and putting it in a trunk. Other than the ornamental table, there was no other furniture of our own to be moved. I took down the miniature of Charles from above my bedside, wrapped it in a shawl and placed it in the trunk. Charles, however, would not allow anyone to touch his desk. He personally emptied each of the drawers, packing every item away with the greatest care.

When the driver arrived to transport our belongings, Charles raced down the stairs to instruct him that everything should be loaded in an orderly fashion. I lingered for a moment and took one last look at the room. The framed faces upon the wall looked down upon me kindly and wished me well. They smiled in anticipation of the new occupants, and they were smiling still when I turned and closed the door on my life at Furnival's Inn, forever.

CHAPTER NINE

April 1837
48 Doughty Street, London

The delivery of furniture, rugs, curtains and paintings was announced daily by the frequent ring of the doorbell. Some days these items seemed to arrive faster than they could be put away or arranged and Charles would complain upon his return home that the house looked like a pawnbroker's shop. To my mind it was not a thing to be rushed, the placing of furniture, the hanging of curtains the positioning of paintings, but Charles could not abide disorder; it appeared to distress him deeply and he would complain repeatedly.

'Kate, I thought I had told you yesterday where I wanted the table and chairs.' Or, 'Didn't I say, Kate, that that picture would look well above the fireplace in the sitting room?'

'But, my love,' I would argue, 'it is a huge task to arrange a house, especially with a young child to see to.'

Narrowly avoiding a collision with a potted plant, Charles exploded.

'For heaven's sake, Kate! There are to be no more excuses. You have Cook and Emily to assist you now and you could call upon that young brother of mine. He cannot seem to find gainful employment. Surely he could do some of the lifting and moving for you?'

Young Fred Dickens had become such a regular visitor to our

home, that I had set aside a bedroom especially for him.

'You should not encourage him, Kate. He should be out seeking work, not idling his hours away at my expense.'

I defended Fred saying that as we did not have a male servant, he was such a help to us, sharpening knives, seeing to the garden. But, in truth, Fred spent his days teasing Cook and Emily, smoking Charles's cigars and drinking his brandy. I often had to send out to replenish supplies before his irascible brother returned from work. But how could one reprove him? Fred filled the house with laughter and mischief and was such good company when Charles was away all day.

In sharp contrast to the trail of impedimenta littered over the three storeys was Charles's study. He had spent hours positioning and repositioning his desk, setting out his writing implements and arranging his growing library of books. Within two days of our arrival at Doughty Street, the room shone as a very model of good order and was now strictly out of bounds to the servants. Even I had taken to knocking tentatively before going in there.

Cook and Emily had been a real blessing. Cook, sensing that I was not organized by nature, instinctively knew where a tactful suggestion would be welcomed, and yet, it was always offered with the utmost respect and humility. Emily had taken to her duties well, thankfully with little direction needed from me. Cook put her right when necessary and had no doubt taken on the role of a maternal figure to the young girl.

Sensing the return of my own equanimity, baby Charles had become a contented little soul and had settled down into a healthy pattern of feeding and sleeping. Georgina loved him like her own little doll and walked him about the garden whenever she visited. I had become more used to Charles's mercurial temperament and as for Mary, well, Mary continued to bless everything and everyone with her gentle air of calmness. Life in the Dickens household was good.

One evening in May, Charles returned home and announced that he was taking us all to the theatre. Fred who had been on the verge of making a hasty exit due to the fact that he had smoked Charles's last cigar, suddenly decided that his misdemeanour might not be discovered after all and concluded that he too would enjoy an evening's entertainment if his brother were paying. We strolled across the City passing a dingy collection of pie shops, butchers and old book stalls. The smell of cooked beef emanated from a coaching inn and Charles noticed a small boy who was being carried over his father's shoulder and the look of hunger which was etched into his features. Charles glanced down at the bag of ripe cherries which he held in his hand and, all at once, a look of compassion crossed his face. He followed behind and began to offer the cherries to the child, one by one, to the complete ignorance of the parent.

Coming to the better part of town, we walked past Billington's London Warehouse, where Mary and I had spent many a happy hour looking at fans, gloves, bonnets, jewellery and the large selection of muslins. It had now closed for the day but Mary and I admired the display in the large square windows through which we could see a young woman polishing the oak counters. We continued along the busy streets until at last we came to King Street.

The St James's theatre was newly built at the expense of a Mr John Branham. Mr Branham managed the theatre and performed there often himself, being a very fine singer. He had asked Charles to write and direct some comedy sketches and he frequently conferred with Charles for advice on a variety of stage productions. Charles delighted in the theatre and his favourite actor was William Charles Macready who had recently performed Shakespeare to critical acclaim. Charles admired his work greatly and soon the two had become friends. I had met Mrs Macready and liked her a good deal, although I always felt a little timid in her husband's company. His sonorous voice was quite alarming!

After the performance, the four of us crossed the town once more and took a leisurely walk home. I recalled a similar occasion only two years before, when I had been short-tempered with Mary and felt jealous of her. How foolish I had been to misinterpret Charles's feelings for her. I smiled at the recollection, feeling glad that I had left such childishness behind and was now a grown woman with better sense. Fred and Mary walked side by side and laughed together, and I wondered if perhaps one day there might ever be more to their friendship. When we arrived home, Fred was still making jokes, but Mary had become unusually quiet. She politely excused herself, saying that she was tired and bade us all goodnight. Her slender figure alighted the stairs and, as she ascended, I had no idea that it was the last vision I would have of her alive.

A few moments later, we heard a loud crash in her room and Charles and Fred bounded up the stairs in fright, calling her name. I followed behind less nimbly but what I saw upon reaching the bedroom door stilled my heart. Charles was kneeling on the floor and holding Mary in his arms. He whispered softly to her, his tears falling upon her face. One of her shoes dangled from her foot and Charles gently replaced it and stroked her cheek.

'Dearest Mary, don't worry, I am here. I shall not leave you.'

Fred paced the room and wrung his hands, not at all sure what to do until I implored him to quickly go for Dr Bell. When he returned, Charles was still cradling Mary in his arms. The doctor retrieved his stethoscope from his bag and encouraged Charles to lay Mary upon the bed so that he might examine her. But Charles refused and held onto her more than ever. A moment later, after a brief examination, the doctor put his stethoscope away and placed a hand upon Charles's shoulder.

'I am sorry, sir, it is too late. She has already gone. You must put her down now, there's a good fellow.'

'No!' Charles cried. 'You are wrong. She is only sleeping. She took a little brandy from my own hand, not a few moments before you came.'

'Believe me, sir, it is of no use. We can do no more.'

Doctor Bell tried to coax him into releasing her, but to no avail. Charles began to sob and called her name over and over, until his voice became a hoarse whisper, 'Mary, oh Mary, please do not leave me. I shall not be able to face the world if you are not in it.'

Her countenance was as beautiful as it had ever been and it held a look of sad apology upon it. As in life, so in death, Mary had not wanted to cause distress to anyone. The delicate hands that had always been quick to come to the aid of others, hung at her side in limp inactivity. But it was her eyes that were the most painful to behold. They were vacant, the laughter and joy which had animated her spirit, completely absent. She looked past us all: we had faded from her life and she from ours.

When Mama arrived, she went into hysterics, Fred had hidden himself away unable to see his brother in such a state of despair and I had no time to think of my own grief being in complete shock at all that was happening around me. Papa remained courageous and strong. He ordered the printing of funeral cards to be distributed to family and friends and purchased mourning clothes and gloves for Mama and me.

On the day of the funeral the sun was clear and bright, the birds rejoiced and every flower in the garden bloomed. It was as though nature was mirroring Mary's own joy at living. But Mary lay still and lifeless in her coffin and it was more than flesh and blood could bear to see her so. As she was lowered into her grave, Charles bowed his head, his frame broken with grief.

The journey home from the cemetery was wordless as there seemed nothing to own that had any meaning. When we entered Doughty Street and closed the door behind us, Charles broke the silence. He carefully removed his gloves, finger by finger as if numbering off each of the things he had to say.

'Catherine' – his manner was aloof – 'under no circumstance should anything in Mary's room be removed. Do you understand? Nothing at all.'

'Yes, Charles, but—'

'And I shall be going into the City later to see my lawyer. I have decided to alter my will. I want it known that upon my death I wish to be buried beside Mary.'

'Your lawyer. . . ?'

'Yes, my lawyer, now I have nothing further to say on the matter, Catherine. Please leave, I wish to be left alone.'

'But Charles, I—'

'Alone I said!'

In the days that followed he did not eat, or work, but sat in a fireside chair staring into space, not speaking at all. I noticed that he was wearing upon his little finger a ring which he had taken from Mary's hand, and he twisted it unconsciously back and forth, lost in his thoughts. Rumours abounded that Charles had gone mad, hence his absence in print and, as I could not seem to bring him comfort nor consolation, Papa, in a bid to restore him to his senses, arranged for us to return to the cottage in Chalk. At first Charles was reluctant, but Papa encouraged him to go saying that it would do him good. In my own despair, I miscarried a child, but I spoke nothing of it to Charles, fearing that his sanity could bear no further loss.

CHAPTER TEN

July 1837
48 Doughty Street, Holborn

One morning, a few weeks after Mary's death, I took the unusual step of disturbing Charles in his study. He had continued to be distant and withdrawn, losing himself completely in his work. I knocked upon the door and called his name tentatively. When I entered at his bidding, he left off writing and looked up with an air of weariness, his face pale and his eyes ringed with dark shadows. He put down his pen with a heavy sigh.

'Kate, I'm glad that you're here. I have something to tell you.'

His voice held a note of seriousness that alarmed me.

'I have decided to distance myself for a little while from everything that has happened in this house. I plan to spend some time in France and Belgium – no doubt the change of scene will do me good.'

He opened the drawer of his desk and became preoccupied with arranging the items within it.

My voice wavered, 'Am I not to come with you?'

He did not reply and I was unsure as to whether he had heard me or if he was deep in thought.

'Charles?'

He slammed the drawer shut and pushed his fingers through his hair, gripping it as he spoke. 'God's truth, Kate! Don't you realize, that everyone wants so much of me that I shall go insane if I do not have some time alone?'

His voice quivered with anger.

I wanted to remind him that I was grieving too; the house was so empty without Mary and if he were to leave me also then I would be completely alone. But I knew from experience that if I were to display even a hint of complaint in my response, he would explode. So I put my feelings to one side saying, 'Very well, my love, if that is what you must do then I shall not make it difficult for you, even though it will be very hard for me.'

I stood for a moment, waiting for some sign of gratitude or acknowledgement, but instead, he picked up his pen, dipped it in the inkwell and became engrossed once more in his writing. It was as if I was not there at all.

I tried not to make a great display of tears when he left for Europe, but turning back into the house, all at once it felt so large and empty without his great personality to fill it. So I quickly decided that I must keep busy while he was away and that I would seek to improve myself. Whereas Charles had grown in fame, I felt insignificant beside him and, as he worked to improve his own knowledge, the space between our abilities grew ever more apparent. So I resolved to apply myself to learn a little French and Italian in the hope that when he travelled abroad again he might take me with him without shame.

Isabella recommended a Mr Francis Smith, her sister's tutor, to assist me. I felt quite nervous upon our first meeting and I feared that he might find me lacking as a student. He was a tall, slim young man with dark curly hair not unlike Charles's, but that was where any similarity ended. He was of a quiet and tranquil temperament and he appeared to have endless patience no matter how much I struggled to grasp what he taught me. He was liberal with his praise and I quickly came to crave the approbation that he so readily bestowed. In addition, I practised the piano as I had not done in a long time and I set about writing down a few recipes with the idea that Charles might assist me to get them published upon his return.

Mr Smith called each day. I learned that he had been sadly widowed last spring and was left with a young son, Theo, to care for.

'You must bring the dear little fellow to tea,' I invited, and Mr Smith accepted with alacrity.

But it was an invitation that I came to regret as the boy did not prove to be 'a dear little fellow' at all. It appeared that he had been completely spoilt by his maternal grandmother who had nursed him with misplaced leniency, causing him to become entirely ill-disciplined. On arrival, the child wore a sullen expression, which I had mistaken for grief at the loss of his mother. But when tea was brought in, his expression changed to one of greedy delight and his poor father was frustrated in his endeavours to control the boy as he took cake before sandwiches, bounced restlessly upon the couch and spoke with a full mouth, showering crumbs everywhere. I was not at all inclined to repeat the invitation and, thankfully, Mr Smith did not ask that I might do so.

At the end of August my husband returned and he was pleased to note my accomplishments.

'Well done, Kate!' he beamed with delight when I greeted him in Italian. 'I am pleased to see that you have not idled your time away.'

Charles also demonstrated that his attention had returned to family life.

Taking a flower from the garden, he inhaled its scent deeply and fixed it into his button hole.

'I have been thinking that we might go away together, Kate, and perhaps your mama and little Georgina could accompany us.'

Mama had still not recovered from the shock of Mary's death and I knew that it would do her good to get away.

'But let us not be too sombre, eh, Kate? Let's take young Frederick with us; he will keep us in a merry mood.'

We rented a small two-storey cottage in Broadstairs, a quiet fishing village in Kent. Charles loved it there, the ebb and flow of the sea appeared to inspire and move him greatly. In the evenings we would gather around him and listen as he read out a scene from his latest novel, *Oliver Twist*. The blood-curdling screams that accompanied the death of poor Nancy had us all gripped with fear and afterwards Charles's eyes twinkled with amusement at the power which he held over us. By day Charles walked along the beach and sometimes he would allow me to accompany him if I promised not to interrupt his flow of thought. With great difficulty I endeavoured to match his energetic strides and keep pace with him.

I reflected how I had seen him go through so many changes since that first meeting in Mama and Papa's drawing room. It was as though his traits had become more exaggerated with the growth of his fame. He had always been of an orderly disposition, but of late he had taken to frequently checking and combing his hair as if he could not even bear disorder upon his head. His taste in clothes now verged on the outrageous; his brightly coloured waistcoats and cravats often drawing a raised eyebrow from passers-by. But since Mary's death, the change that was hardest to bear was that he had developed a veneer of detached composure as if he feared being held captive to his emotions. It seemed as if Mary's death had done more than bereave him, it had warned him that never again could he allow anything to rob him of his sanity or the vital energy that he needed in order to make a living.

When we returned to Doughty Street he filled the house with as many visitors and as much noise as seemed possible, but I felt that all of this was merely a buffer between himself and reality.

CHAPTER ELEVEN

March 1838
The Star and Garter Inn, Richmond

Our baby daughter was born on a bright morning in March. The crocuses and snowdrops were in full bloom and I was delighted that spring was on its way. We agreed to name our pretty daughter Mary and at just a few hours old she lay in her father's arms. He sat at my bedside in a soft leather chair and as he rocked her, the tears fell from his face and splashed onto hers.

'Dear sweet Mary, I believe that so perfect a creature never lived before.'

My heart stilled for a moment – a memory of someone else cradled in those very same arms had come to mind. I looked at the ring upon his little finger, which he had never taken off since the day that my sister had died, and her room and clothing had remained in place just as he had instructed.

'Do you think of her often?' I found myself saying with difficulty.

He nodded sadly and, handing the baby back to me, he moved to the window seat, sat down and sighed deeply.

'I think about her every day and dream of her each night. I do not believe I shall ever leave off missing her until the day that I die.'

He was quiet and still for a moment and then, realizing that he had dropped his guard, he quickly reined in his emotions and pointed out of the window.

'Well, look who's here!' he laughed, 'It's my old friend John Forster, coming to wish us well, no doubt. I'll go down to meet him and see if he would like to take a ride out, I feel like working off some energy.'

He returned to my side, promptly kissed the top of my head and in the same moment was gone. What strange behaviour! I could hardly fathom it out. It was hard to believe that beneath such a cheery exterior, he was hiding so much pain.

As he left, Fanny entered the room and my spirits sank. Wherever Fanny went, a headache was not far behind and it usually seemed to attach itself to me. She looked at me with disapproval.

'That husband of yours has something on his mind, I'll wager. He has an air of melancholy about him, don't you think? I expect it's the baby's name, t'would remind him of your sister. My, what a pretty maid she was! Such a terrible loss for him. Don't think he'll ever get over it.'

Fanny's attention then turned to the confusion of clutter about the bedroom. Unfinished mending on the chair, a litter of letters upon the dressing table, hairpins, hatpins, powders, perfume bottles.

'Goodness, Kate, 'tis a wonder that you can find the little one amongst all of this lot. My brother always did like orderliness, you know, it quiets his mind.'

I finally found my voice. 'Fanny, please! You are speaking out of turn.'

'Well, somebody has to say it and it might as well be me. You should have a tighter rein on matters, Kate, Charles cannot see to the home as well as earning a living, you know. Your sister would have never allowed the house to fall into such disarray.'

I felt my body tense with resentment. In life my sister had outshone me: in death she eclipsed me still.

The following month Charles and I celebrated our second wedding anniversary and I felt well enough to travel to

Richmond for a few days. We planned to stay at the Star and Garter and as our carriage took a track through the Petersham meadows, our accommodation came into view. I marvelled at the exterior which looked just like the home of a nobleman. Charles told me that the inn was built on a site which dated back to Charles I.

While our bags were unloaded, Charles nodded at the upstairs window and said, with a twinkle in his eye, 'Did you know, Kate, that the wife of the former owner is said to haunt the corridors at night? Her husband was reputed to have been a foolish man who made costly additions to the property and died in prison without a penny to his name.'

'Stop it, Charles.' I giggled nervously. 'How do you expect me to sleep if you tell me such things?'

A few days later we were joined by Charles's friend, Forster, who excitedly told us that the first edition of Charles's latest work, *Nicholas Nickleby*, had sold 50,000 copies.

'No need to hide yourself away here, Dickens! It's good news all round.'

Charles was developing the habit of avoiding reviews for fear that they may dispirit him, but Forster waved a copy of the morning paper under his nose and insisted, 'Read that, dear fellow. The editor, Lord Jeffrey, has nothing but praise for you.'

He also pulled from his pocket a crumpled note which he handed to Charles with a grin. 'And this is from one of your younger admirers.'

Charles looked puzzled and opened up the note and began to read. A few moments later his face broke out into a smile, followed by a laugh which grew louder and louder until the tears rolled down his cheeks.

Forster joined in, 'It's priceless, isn't it, my friend?'

It appeared that a little boy had written stating his views as to the rewards and punishments that should me meted out upon the various characters in Charles's story.

'What a capital little fellow he must be, I will reply immediately. Lord Jeffrey will have to wait!'

It was wonderful to witness that my husband, in spite of his growing fame, should choose to acknowledge the words of a young child above that of a well-known literary critic.

In June our new sovereign Queen Victoria was crowned. The monarchy had fallen out of favour in recent years but almost everyone was won over by the tiny princess who would become our new Queen. Crowds flocked to London for the coronation and it was estimated that there were half a million strangers in London and a room could not be found for love nor money. Charles was excited to attend.

'Come with me, Kate, why don't you?'

But I was not inclined to be jostled by crowds of well-wishers and said that I would prefer instead the quietness of my own home. A look of disappointment fell across Charles's face and for a moment I felt guilty as he closed the door to leave. But the peace that I had imagined did not come at all, instead being intermittently broken by the firing of distant cannon, incessant ringing of bells and a twenty-one gun salute. Day turned into night and the celebratory fireworks punctuated the darkness of the City.

When Charles returned he told me that the procession from Buckingham Palace had been led by trumpeters, life guards and a marching band, and although he had not been able to catch a glimpse of the royal carriage, he had heard that the Queen's head was crowned with diamonds and that she wore a crimson cape trimmed with ermine. The next day reports of the coronation filled the pages of the newspapers. Charles perused the *Morning Chronicle* over his breakfast and then I noticed that he studied one section of print very carefully, 'Well, I never!' he whispered, and discreetly wiped a tear from his eye.

'Listen to this, Kate. It says here that when one of the elderly lords took the steps to pay homage to the Queen he fell and rolled right down the steps to the throne. In fear that the old man might be hurt, the Queen advanced and took his arm to aid him to his feet.'

His face shone with delight. 'I think that we should not underestimate the diminutive size of our little sovereign. I think that she has the determination to shape our world in ways yet unknown.'

CHAPTER TWELVE

August 1838
Coutts and Company, The Strand

Not far from Holborn, in the Strand, is a fine-looking banking establishment known as Coutts and Company. Designed by the architect John Nash, its entrance reminds an imaginative onlooker of two pepper pots side by side. Within the grand walls, sits a row of clerks, each one behind his mahogany desk, over which money and gold change hands in the most dignified manner. Acting upon the advice of John Forster, Charles met Mr Edward Marjoribanks, a partner in the bank and opened an account there. The sum deposited was a nominal amount and so Charles was surprised to be afforded the courtesies of an old and valued client. Upon hearing that London's well-known author had become a customer, Miss Angela Burdett-Coutts seized the chance of an introduction.

Miss Burdett-Coutts's grandfather had had no sons and neither had her late mother. Consequently the lady had recently found herself heiress to a sizeable fortune. My husband was most impressed to find that at the age of twenty-four, she had just one great wish: to use her wealth to help the less fortunate. After their first meeting, Charles arrived home full of excitement and enthusiasm. I was sitting at my needlework when he burst into the room with the words, 'Kate, I have just met the most marvellous woman! We really must invite her to our home.'

I felt myself prickle with resentment and stopped my sewing mid-stitch.

'What do you mean – the most marvellous woman?'

He paced the room energetically, slapping his gloves upon his hands.

'She's got money, Kate, lots of it. But she has resolved to share it with the less fortunate in society. Isn't that wonderful?'

'I don't see what that has got to do with us,' I said, resuming my stitching.

Charles fell upon one knee and stilled my work with his hand.

'But don't you see? She has access to money that can fund my ideas for social reform.'

In his earnestness he caught his finger upon my needle and I watched with dismay as a drop of blood fell and spread into a crimson stain upon my cross-stitch.

'Oh, Charles!' I cried in exasperation. 'Look what you have done now.'

A look of hurt and disappointment fell across his face.

'Well, perhaps if you showed a little more interest in what I had to tell you, it wouldn't have happened.' And with an air of dejection he left the room.

It was true, I had no interest in social matters whatsoever. Of course I felt sorry for those in the workhouse, for children who had to labour under terrible conditions and for those who did not know where their next meal was coming from. But these were issues that I preferred not to dwell upon. I found it all too depressing. Yet, if I was to keep my husband's favour then I knew I must show greater support for his interests. I put my sewing to one side and sought him out.

I found him in the sitting room, angrily prodding the hot coals with a poker.

'Charles, I am sorry. You are right. If Miss Burdett-Coutts is as generous as you say, then, of course, you must invite her to our home and see what she can help you to accomplish.'

He did not reply, but stared at the fire with a sullen expression upon his face.

I put my hand upon his arm. 'Charles? Please don't be cross. I am sorry, truly I am.'

He eyed me with suspicion. 'Are you sure, Kate? Do you really mean it?'

'Yes, of course, my love. I will speak to Mama immediately and see if she will allow me to borrow Alice for the evening.'

Pleased at getting his own way, he forgot his sulkiness, drew me towards him and kissed my forehead.

Miss Burdett-Coutts, escorted by Mr Marjoribanks, arrived half an hour later than expected. She held out her hand and greeted me with an apology.

'Please, will you excuse my tardiness, Mrs Dickens? I was detained at my lawyer's office. He is handling the purchase of a property for me, a little project that I have in mind to discuss with your husband later.'

I examined her face carefully as she spoke. It was long and narrow, the features being not in the least bit beautiful, except for her eyes, which were full of kindness and shone with sincerity. She wore a deep cream-silk evening dress with short puffed sleeves and, as she moved from the hall to the dining room, I caught the light scent of jasmine and lavender.

Over dinner she and Charles engaged in animated conversation and I could see why Charles was taken with her. She was intelligent, witty and possessed an enthusiasm for life that matched his own. She nodded as she listened to his lively discourse. Earlier in the year, Charles had visited Yorkshire and been most distressed at the terrible conditions that existed in the schools there. The pupils were ill-treated, malnourished and were subjected to the most cruel punishments. Miss Burdett-Coutts was fascinated by Charles's yearning to cover the subject in his writing.

'What a wonderful idea, Mr Dickens, that is just what is needed – a greater awareness of such matters.'

She, in turn, quietly confided her own plans to open a hostel for fallen women. Mr Marjoribanks, who had appeared to be absorbed in conversing with John Forster about investments, turned his head quickly and, with a disapproving frown, interjected, 'I am not sure that the partners at the bank would approve of you using your allowance to fund such a project, miss.'

But it seemed that Angela Burdett-Coutts was not a woman to be held back by the opinion of any man and she laughed good-naturedly. 'Those elderly gentleman have quickly given up telling me how I should use my money, my dear Mr M, and I hope that you will soon tire of it too.'

I marvelled at her words and could not help but envy her a little: she did not seem to be bound at all by the conventions that governed most women, but appeared to be completely independent in both mind and action.

As the evening progressed, laughter filled the candlelit dining room. Charles dropped into his chair, exhausted from recounting a humorous sketch in which he had taken all the parts.

'My dear boy, what a marvellous actor you are!' Forster whooped, clapping his hands.

Mr Marjoribanks enthused with wonder, 'You are outshone by no other, sir!'

Miss Burdett-Coutts nodded, joining in the applause and Forster raised his glass in a toast.

'There is little chance that you will ever return to the blacking factory now, dear fellow, you can be sure of that.'

His ever-ready lips were pursed to take another swig of wine but above the rim he saw an unexplained fierceness enter into Charles's eyes. My husband leaned across the table and fixed Forster with a glare.

'That,' he hissed, 'is a part of my life that I wish never to be mentioned.'

The room fell silent. Forster cleared his throat and attempted a gay little laugh to lighten the atmosphere. 'Come now, Dickens, no offence intended. It was the wine, you know, loosened my tongue, old chap.'

I looked from one to the other.

'What is he talking about, Charles? When did you ever work in such an awful place?'

Charles brought down his fist upon the table, jolting the cutlery to life.

'Never to be mentioned, I said!'

In an effort to calm the situation, I stood up and said with a nervous smile, 'Gentlemen, whatever secrets have passed between you, let us not spoil a delightful evening. Allow me to call in the dessert.'

Forster leaned to one side and hiccupped into Marjoribank's ear, 'I mean, I'm his dearest friend, so what is there to be ashamed of?'

Charles pushed back his chair and roared, pointing his finger at the door, 'Out! I want you out of this house. How dare you come here and humiliate me?'

'But, Dickens—' Forster began.

'I said out, and I mean out, sir. Do I have to remove you by my own hand in order to make myself clear?'

At this Forster took exception and, holding onto the table to steady himself, he stood to his feet, swaying slightly. His unsteady grasp on the table tore at the cloth, bringing plates and cutlery crashing to the floor.

'Have you come so far in this world, Dickens, that you cannot take a joke at your own expense?'

Charles stood up and made towards Forster in an attempt to carry out his word to remove him, but Edward Marjoribanks, fearing that blows were about to be exchanged, stood between them. 'Gentlemen, please!'

Unable to witness any more, I ran from the room in tears: the best of friends at war and a wonderful dinner party ruined! Still, the voices grew louder until the angry words reached a climax and were abruptly silenced by a loud bang and the smashing of glass. I came from the sitting room where I had been pacing up and down in tearful agitation, and found the hallway littered with fragments of glass and a broken pane in the front door.

Forster had left. Whether voluntarily or aided by my husband I did not know.

Mr Marjoribanks and Miss Burdett-Coutts hovered by the door, not at all sure what to say in the way of a farewell. A strained smile passed between the three of us.

'I'm so very sorry. . . .' I apologized.

Miss Burdett-Coutts moved towards me awkwardly as if to demonstrate a gesture of condolence, but thought the better of it and, clearing her throat, dropped her hand saying, 'Well, goodnight then, madam,' and hastily departed with Marjoribanks at her side.

Cook came into the hallway and, upon seeing the glass, whispered, 'I will fetch a pan and brush, madam.'

I glanced anxiously at the dining-room door.

'Please, Cook, no. Wait until the master has gone to bed.'

Hearing the door open, Cook and I darted back into the sitting room, knowing only too well to keep out of Charles's way when he was angry. However, he did not ascend the stairs to bed as I had expected, but instead opened the front door, snatched up his cane and went out into the foggy night without hat, scarf or coat. It was not at all unusual for him to walk in the darkness of the city, ruminating and creating his works of fiction, but tonight was different; tonight he was angry and the night was shrouded in a heavy mist, a hiding place for danger. I prayed that no one would confront him for in this mood he was certainly ready to cause injury. Where was he going? He was surely not off to finish his argument with Forster?

What fools men were. Forster might be loud and irritating, I acknowledged that, but the sincerity of his friendship with my husband could not be called into question by anyone. They had first met through a journalist friend of my father's and had quickly found out how many interests they shared: a love of literature and the arts, a passion for political reform and an inclination towards tomfoolery. When it came to matters of business, however, Forster had a sound mind and quickly set about giving my husband valuable advice and representing him in legal concerns. From that first meeting they had become inseparable and, although at times I found Forster boorish and overbearing, I could never have wished such an awful argument to come between them.

Charles had still not returned long after midnight and I lay in bed, drifting in and out of a restless sleep, imagining him lying in a gutter somewhere, his throat slit and his pockets emptied. The click of the bedroom door startled me and I awoke. Charles had returned. I thanked God that he was safe and yet something held me back from embracing him or speaking. He undressed in the darkness and slipped into the bed next to me without a word. He turned on his side, buried his head in his pillow and to my alarm began to weep.

'What have I done? Forster will never forgive me. Never. I have lost the dearest friend I ever had. And Miss Burdett-Coutts, she will think me completely ill-bred.'

I resisted the temptation to reach out my hand to him, knowing that he would not want me to see him this way. Despite his terrible anger, his regret was now plain to see.

CHAPTER THIRTEEN

September 1838
The Thames, London

In the weeks that followed, Charles suffered with a bad cold, the result of his night-time excursion. He was plagued by facial spasms and was in a terrible mood: either completely silent, not speaking at all, or anxious and irritable. I did not dare to ask him a word about Forster. It was the arrival of a letter requesting his help that at last lifted him out of his gloom. After reading it carefully, he folded it in two and hurried to his study to make a reply.

My Dear Miss Burdett-Coutts

I am honoured to place myself at your disposal, and will do all that you ask of me and more, if I can, to assist the young woman in question. I will gladly arrange the passage as you have asked and take the ticket to her.

Your sister shows the same charitable spirit as yourself in what she does for these young women. You are right when you say that we must not sit in judgement, but that those of us that have the means to help, must do so.

I await your further instructions.

Your sincere friend,
Charles Dickens

Within our huge City there were often unmarried women who found themselves with child. Cast out, their only refuge was the workhouse, which was often a sure passage to death for mother or child, sometimes both. Angela Burdett-Coutts, I learned, had a sister who had emigrated to Australia and had set up a hostel for these poor unfortunates. Here they could start a new life, away from a hypocritical society, and find hope of a better future.

Charles later told me how he had wandered down to the docks.

'Do you know, Kate, I passed children as young as two years old, picking their way through stinking rubbish in the hope of finding food. It was heartbreaking to see.'

In the loft of a dilapidated boathouse he had found the girl. She was no more than sixteen and was huddled beneath a fraying sackcloth. Her fair hair hung about her delicate face like rats' tails.

'Who told you I was 'ere?' she had called fearfully. 'Keep away from me, or I'll skin you wiv' me knife.' She shuffled back into the corner and flashed the blade in warning.

'I won't harm you, little miss,' Charles had reassured. 'I've come to help. I heard what happened to you.'

The girl held up a lantern, seeking sincerity in her visitor's eyes.

'I know that you had a good position until your master's son brought these circumstances upon you.'

The girl nodded cautiously, 'Sir Robert Bradbury-Kent's son, up at the big house on Upper Thames Street.'

Charles knew the family. Generations of money had not instilled good character in any of them, it had only robbed them of morals and filled them with arrogance instead.

'I have something for you,' said Charles, crouching down and moving a little closer. He had held out a ticket and a small purse of money. The girl eyed him suspiciously.

'A lady will meet you at the railway station tomorrow at eight, under the station clock. You must not speak to her or appear to accompany her, but she will be your silent chaperon on the train journey. She will be wearing a green velvet bonnet. When you arrive at the docks a ship will be waiting, bound for Australia. Here is your passage.' Charles had said, holding out the ticket.

The girl held back, not convinced, 'Why are you doin' this? Wot's in it for you? You don't know me at all. I could run away wiv that money and sell the ticket for a good price, you know that don't ya?' She rubbed a dirty hand back and forth across her nose.

'That is your choice of course, little miss, but there will be small chance for you here in London.'

The girl had hesitated for a moment, not at all sure if she could ever trust another man, then cautiously got to her feet and took a step towards Charles. The fragile creature did not have any idea at all that she stood before a famous author, but looked into his kind eyes and recognized that they swam with tears of pity. She snatched the ticket and the bag of coins from Charles's hand and then made a quick retreat to her bed of sacking.

Charles bid her goodbye and then turned to leave. She whispered softly, 'Mister? If I should survive, then I will always remember your kindness, but if I should die, then I will ask God in person to bless you for what you have done.'

'It is the lady and her sister that you have to thank, I am just their errand boy.' He smiled. 'But all that will become known to you when you reach the other side of the world.' He shook her tiny hand and they said goodbye.

Walking past the little children by the docks once more, he resolved to see what could be done for them. He would speak to Miss Burdett-Coutts about it. Charles had seen the letter from her as a sign of her continued good will, and that she had not forsaken him after all. This was the first of many occasions when he worked with Angela Burdett-Coutts in her acts of charity. Sometimes he would receive word of how the lives of the young women he helped her to support, had turned out and it would always lift his mood, knowing that he had been able to make a small difference by doing some social good.

CHAPTER FOURTEEN

October 1839
Devonshire Terrace, The Regent's Park

Before the wheels of the carriage had hardly stopped turning, Charles threw open the door and jumped down onto the road, gesturing excitedly at the large town house before us.

'This is it, Kate! This is it! The very house that I have told you so much about.'

We had driven west of Doughty Street leaving behind us the courts and alley-ways of Holborn, the muddy thoroughfares that echoed with the shouts of street vendors selling dog collars, birds, books, sticks, tracts, herbs, spices, crockery – in fact every manner of wares that a person might want or need – until the street became a little less dusty and we turned into the Tottenham Court Road with its well-dressed shop windows and recently swept pavements. Presently we arrived in a newly developed and respectable part of town close to The Regent's Park.

'Wait until you see inside, it is truly magnificent.' Charles said breathlessly. With only a few weeks to go until the arrival of our third child, I was a little slower about my step and, with the help of the driver, I made a wary descent from the carriage. Charles had already run up the steps and was remonstrating with the keys to the front door, which appeared to be rather stiff and unyielding in the lock.

'Will – you – turn!' Charles gritted his teeth, determined not to be mastered.

'Charles, if you force it, the key will break.'

'Yes, I am very well aware of that, my dear, thank you!'

With a sharp upward exhalation he blew a curl away from his perspiring brow, and tried once more, this time with success.

'There!'

The door swung open to reveal a large hall with black-and-white tiling.

'It's very grand, Charles,' I acknowledged, with a little awe.

'Just so! Just so! Am I not a famous author now? Macready has a place not far from here, you know, but not as big as this, Kate. Nowhere near as big as this.'

Our family was growing and our current home was undoubtedly becoming too small for us, but Charles felt the need to prove himself an equal among his contemporaries, and there was little doubt that this mansion would enable him to do just that. He had been hunting for a new home for weeks and had precise requirements in mind: a street not too wide or too narrow and free of traders and street entertainers, and a house well lit by sunshine with plenty of large windows. He had consulted a surveyor to ensure that the basement was not damp and a lawyer to ensure that there were no unpaid bills attached to the property. With all these requirements satisfied, he had settled upon Devonshire Terrace.

Charles took me by the hand and led me into one of the rooms.

'Close your eyes, Kate, I have something to show you. Now, open!'

I opened my eyes with great expectation and was instantly disappointed to see before me a large, dusty, empty room; but with eyes full of imagination, Charles saw so much more.

'This, Kate, will be the library.' he said with pride. He walked the length of the extensive room, his footsteps echoing upon the wooden floor, his mind running ahead to the finished project. 'I will have the walls fitted from floor to ceiling with oak shelves, and I will have the works of Shakespeare here, the Greek poets there; Wordsworth, Shelley and Keats.' He pointed as if slotting each book into place, '*Don Quixote, Robinson Crusoe, Gulliver's Travels* – all of them Kate, all of them! Including every damn book that my father ever took from me. It will be a library to envy.'

'Well, if it will make you happy, my love,' I demurred.

His face changed to one of earnestness, 'But are *you* happy, Kate?'

Disappointed by my muted response he muttered under his breath, 'I suppose that it is too much to expect that we should both be happy at the same time!'

'Charles, I only. . . .'

But he had gone, bounding up the stairs to inspect the bedrooms. He didn't seem to understand that I lived my life quietly, not one to be excited by strong emotion nor unduly moved by the routine changes that life brought.

That night Charles was late at his desk and I drifted in and out of a shallow sleep, aware that at that very desk he was not writing with ease and enjoyment, but was sweating, striving, struggling, wrestling to give birth to every word he inscribed. He was fidgety, flustered, restless and irritable and when at last he came to bed the restlessness crept into his dreams and prodded and plagued him, until he awoke with a start.

'*Where is she? Where has she gone?*'

'Hush, my love, you are dreaming, you are just dreaming.'

'The midwife.' he explained, gripping his hair. 'I was dreaming that she had gone to the wrong house. . . .'

'But the baby is not here yet, Charles.'

I stroked his hair, trying to soothe away his terrors and he took my hand and held his lips against it for a moment.

'I must go and work, Kate, my mind is awake.'

'No, Charles, please. You are overtired, you need to rest.'

But he had already swung his legs out of bed and was pulling his dressing-gown about him. His publisher was pressing him to finish his current novel, but poor Charles was struggling to keep up, as he was writing and editing for a weekly magazine too, and in agonies deliberating over the illustrations for his novel. I worried that he was doing too much.

Conscious of my husband's heavy workload, I dedicated my time to organizing the house move. The days were filled with packing, sorting, discarding, gathering and parcelling up. But one thought gnawed at my mind, bit by bit eating away at my equanimity until I could bear it no longer: *what should I do about Mary's room?* Not one possession of hers had been moved since the day of her death, not one item of clothing, knick-knack or ornament. Her room had become a shrine, so how would Charles react if I touched anything? I was prepared for his anger, but what about his grief? Could I bear that again? But I could not allow these unruly thoughts to paralyse me. With a decisive tone I called to Emily, my hand resting upon the door handle to Mary's room. She responded to my call quickly and came up the stairs at once, but when she saw my intentions, a look of consternation crossed her face.

'But Mr Dickens, ma'am. . . .'

'I know, Emily, please don't worry. I will take full responsibility.'

'Well, if you are sure, madam.'

I took a deep breath and opened the door.

A single white sheet covered the bed like a shroud and the headboard stood guard above it like a tombstone. I shuddered at the image and quickly pushed it from my mind, knowing that if I lingered over the task that lay ahead that I would not see it through. The ornamental fan that Mary had taken to the theatre the night that she died, lay just where she had left it upon the dusty dressing table. Oh, how I wished that she would take it in her hand once more, and laugh and chatter as she did. Dresses, shoes and hats were quickly packed into a chest and when we closed the lid, it felt like I was losing her all over again.

When Charles returned I came up the stairs to find him standing at the open door of the empty room, staring into it.

What did he feel? What would he say? He turned to face me and I was startled to note that his eyes were completely empty of all emotion, it was as if he himself were a corpse. Then I understood: he had willed himself to feel nothing, nothing at all. The veil had come down again.

CHAPTER FIFTEEN

Christmas 1839
Devonshire Terrace

The branches were covered with a glittering frost. Charles walked carefully so as not to slip on the hard-packed snow on the garden path. He looked about furtively for a moment and then disappeared into the garden outbuilding. I watched him with curiosity through the drawing-room window.

'I have no idea what your father is up to, my dears, but I think that we are in for a surprise.'

Charley and Mary ran to the window and pressed their noses to the glass, their hot breath momentarily obscuring the view. Charles reappeared carrying a large dome-shaped object covered with a blanket. He looked at the ground beneath his feet with suspicion and tested it warily. With his first step secure he began a cautious return to the house. When the children heard the front door open and the sound of their father stamping the snow and ice from his feet, they ran with excitement to greet him.

'Papa! Papa!'

From the hallway came a blood-curdling screech.

'Helloa, old girl!'

The children froze with fear and returned to my side, hiding their faces in my skirt. I was just about to reprimand their father for scaring them with one of his silly voices when he entered the room and, with a theatrical flourish, unveiled a cage containing a large black raven. It reminded me somewhat of Charles's mother, the way in which it eyed up the room as if it would descend upon anything that took its delight and carry it away with lightning speed. The children forgot their fear and pulled at their father's jacket excitedly.

'Let it out, Papa! Let it out! We want to see it fly.'

Charles opened the cage and the bird hopped out, whereupon it flew to the curtain pole and much to my horror began pecking the fringes of the curtains.

'Charles! Get it down. What on earth possessed you to purchase such a vile creature? Why couldn't you have bought a dove or a canary? At least they are pretty to look at.'

The unwelcome visitor immediately took offence and began to flap its wings angrily, screeching and squawking about the drawing room. 'Canaries and doves are ordinary,' Charles said defensively, 'but *this* is a bird with character. *This* is Grip.'

In recognition of a soul mate, the bird settled on Charles's shoulder and fixed his eye upon me with satisfaction.

'I suspect that you did not know, Kate, that ravens were highly prized by the Romans; they were the pets of Caesars, you know. Now don't be scared, come and stroke him a little. He won't hurt you.'

The children, who were already fussing the bird, chorused in agreement, 'Yes, Mama, do come, he is really rather sweet.'

Full of doubt and reluctance I lifted my hand and, as I did so, in the blink of an eye, he sharply nipped at my finger. The bird let out a throaty laugh and a look of mischief crossed my husband's face, which he quickly disguised with a cough. From that day on their existed a mutual dislike between myself and that vile creature!

The snow melted and was followed by a new year, but it brought with it grievous news that caused Charles great bitterness.

CHAPTER SIXTEEN

February 1840
Devonshire Terrace

In the parish of St George's, Southwark, on the south side of Angel Court and Angel Alley stands the Marshalsea Prison. To the right is the Dog and Bear Inn, frequented by watermen and sailors on leave and next door a brew house that supplies the same. The air, depending on the wind's direction, alternately hangs with the smell of hops or the stench from the choked drains of the prison.

There are only two kinds of prisoner, although their crimes are much the same, the one has faith that liberty will soon be his and this hope colours his cheeks and shines in his eyes; the other is as sallow as a corpse, hope has long since faded, the light in his eyes obscured. Although the prison is surrounded by high external walls, the debtors' families are at liberty to move freely in and out of the jail if they so wish. But almost all prefer the security of those prison walls to the sound to the bailiff's insistent hammer upon the front door of their homestead.

Mr John Dickens was as softly rounded as his wife was sharp and with his cheery smile, he wore about him a permanently optimistic air as if he expected news of his good fortune at any moment. That many years ago he had resided at that very prison in Marshalsea, had not in anyway dismayed him nor swayed him from the conviction that the worst of circumstances could not but be endured if only one remained buoyant. He had been one of the lucky ones.

At this time in our marriage, Charles had remained silent about that period in his family's history and the whole chapter remained shrouded in mystery. But I was to learn more about the horror with which Charles associated it when amongst his morning mail, an unwelcome letter from his publishers arrived.

12 February 1840

Dear Sir

Although it is the most delicate of subjects, we feel it incumbent upon ourselves to inform you of our concerns for your father's financial affairs.

In August of last year, Mr Dickens asked for our help over some trifling difficulty, and we felt that we could not refuse such a small sum of assistance to a relative of our most distinguished client. Three months later, he called upon us again, this time to loan him another fifteen pounds. He earnestly promised to repay it the following month but instead, in December, he asked for a further thirty-five pounds and Mr Hall said that we should let you know; but your father was so sincere in his apology for not paying us back before, that I could not refuse him.

Yesterday, however, he visited our offices as we were closing up for the day and with great distress, revealed to us the full extent of his worries. He told us that he had other creditors, besides ourselves, who were pressing him for payment in the most threatening manner and so in desperation he begged that we allow him to insure his life in our favour for one hundred pounds. He said that if we did not agree by one o'clock today, he would face the most dire circumstances.

We assure you that we have been most discreet about this matter, but as both your publishers and the guardians of your reputation, we feel that we must inform you of our concern.

We await your advice and remain yours most humbly,

Messrs. Chapman and Hall

Charles's fingers curled around the letter and he raised his hands to his face, shaking his head in disbelief.

'No, no. Not again, not again!'

Just as I thought he was about to weep with despair, he brought his fists down upon the breakfast table with great force and shouted, 'That man will bring ruination to this family!'

He pushed his chair back from the table forcefully and made his way into the hall. I trotted behind him anxious to know what had happened.

'What is it, my love?'

'Give him half a chance, and he will be rounding up our possessions to take them to the pawnbrokers,' Charles growled under his breath. 'I will not tolerate it again!'

'Tolerate what, my love? Who is it that has angered you so?'

Charles snatched up his hat and cane from the hat stand.

'Charles! Will you please tell me what is going on?'

But the only reply I received was the decisive bang of the front door.

A week later, to my surprise, Mr and Mrs Dickens were moved with utmost swiftness to Exeter with strict instructions not to return to London under any circumstances. I dared not ask Charles a word about it for, all week whenever I tried to engage him in conversation, he exploded over the smallest matter. It was Fred who told me all.

When Charles had been just twelve years old, his father had been imprisoned in the Marshalsea for unpaid debts and Charles had been sent to work at Warren's Blacking Factory. His father had sold the household belongings and pawned Charles's books, but this was not enough to pay off the creditors. I was appalled to learn that Charles had spent twelve hours a day, pasting labels onto jars and enduring the taunts of the other children, who saw him as 'the little gentleman'. It was only his determination and hard work that had enabled his family to finally return to their home. I was filled with sympathy.

'It must have been terrible for you all, Fred. Do you remember much of it?'

Fred got up from the couch and poured himself a brandy from the decanter on the bureau.

'Not really, I was very young, but I recall the narrow wooden staircase leading to our room . . . and the stench' – he took a gulp of the golden brown liquid – 'the stench was terrible.'

I stood up and placed a comforting hand upon Fred's arm and he was quiet for a moment, before taking two of Charles's cigars from the bureau drawer. One he lit, the other he tucked into his waistcoat pocket for later.

'Now the old chap has been up to his tricks again, Kate. He has borrowed extensively against Charles's name and has received a note of eviction from the landlord. He was a moment away from arrest when my learned brother intervened.'

Fred's voice took on a lighter note. 'But the parents have landed on their feet from what I have heard.' He puffed heartily on his cigar and strolled about the room, giving each piece of furniture a playful tap as he passed it. 'A little cottage with an orchard and a vegetable garden, according to Mother, so they have not come out of it too badly, by all accounts.'

Emily entered the room with a tray and began to lay the table for dinner.

'Any room for one more?' Fred queried, patting his stomach. He winked at Emily, and then nearly choked upon his cigar at the abrupt opening of the door as Charles's brooding presence entered the room.

He threw his younger brother a dark look. 'What are you doing here? I am surprised that you dare to show your face at my table. In point of fact, I'm sick of the sight of all of you!' Fred glanced guiltily at his empty brandy glass on the table and tucked his thumb self-consciously into his waistcoat pocket lest the spare cigar fall out.

'Did it not occur to you, that you should be out working to help pay off our father's debts? Must I alone be always held responsible for bailing him out? In fact, must I alone be responsible for all of you?' His voice was gaining volume now.

Fred chanced a defence, but I quickly interposed, knowing that Charles was not in any mood to be challenged.

'Well, as we are all together,' I began tentatively, 'shall we enjoy Cook's sirloin of beef? I know it's your favourite, dear.'

Charles looked at the table with disgust. 'I've lost my appetite. I'm going to my study to work. After all, someone has to keep a roof over this family's head.'

CHAPTER SEVENTEEN

April 1840
Devonshire Terrace, London

Charles was irritable: he had finished writing the final instalment of *Nicholas Nickleby* and without a project on hand to engage him, he was restless. He had made several false starts upon another novel but could not seem to settle on an idea which excited him, or that he thought would excite his readers. He paced about the sitting room, drumming his fingertips together, his brow furrowed as if he were struggling to think of a specific word that was eluding him. He huffed and sighed, fretted and frowned, voiced an 'aha!' then shook his head vigorously with anger and frustration.

I had seen him like this on many occasions before and knew that when he found what he was searching for the mystery would be unlocked, he would focus his mind upon it with singular determination and hurry away to his study to fix it in ink before it escaped him. But today was not one of those moments and sensing his mounting agitation, I sought to make an exit before he noticed me. Poised to move from my chair, I unwittingly caught his attention.

'Kate,' he sighed, 'must you always wear that grey dress? It makes you look quite a fright.'

I placed a protective hand on my lace collar and brooch.

'I'm sorry, Charles, I thought the collar and brooch relieved its plainness. But I will change, if it pleases you.'

He looked me up and down with distaste. 'Yes, it would please me greatly.'

'Very well, my love, but is anything wrong? You seem—'

Charles turned, his eyes blazing, 'What? What do I seem? Come along, Kate, let me hear your customary perceptiveness.'

My face fell at his biting sarcasm. I knew the cause of it only too well. A royal wedding had taken place some weeks before. Queen Victoria had married her cousin, Prince Albert of Saxe-Coburg-Gotha and Charles had joked that he was completely broken-hearted. At first I had taken his comments in good spirit and when at the dinner parties we attended in the ensuing weeks, he would drink to her health and pronounce himself distressed that she had forsaken him, I would laugh along with the other guests and try to be a good sport. After all, I saw it for what it was, a distraction from his frustration at not being able to write.

Everyone would cheer at the charade and urge him on to greater tomfoolery, and I would endeavour to smile graciously and enter into the fun. But as the weeks went on, Charles did not cease in the masquerade even when it became obvious that his friends had tired of it; and I found it all the more embarrassing when I overheard hushed whispers from around the dinner table and received nods of sympathy. It seemed that Charles had convinced himself the joke was true. Why shouldn't the Queen return his admiration, he reasoned? Wasn't he every bit her equal in fame and in popularity? Didn't he deserve a woman of title and renown as his companion? In consequence, he became increasingly cold and distant towards me.

One evening, he lay in bed and, staring up at the ceiling, he addressed me.

'You wouldn't understand what it is, Kate, to know greatness. She was born to it: I have had it thrust upon me. We would have so much in common.' He sighed deeply. 'If only we could meet. I have heard that she admires me greatly; oh yes, it is true that she has copies of my work within the very walls of Windsor Castle.'

He paused for a moment as if struck by a new thought. 'Perhaps I should go to Windsor and seek an introduction. She will know I am sincere in my admiration then!'

He punched his pillow, and turned his back upon me in a gesture of indifference. All that I could do was to endure it. Surely it must pass soon. But which woman has ever had a queen as her rival in love?

July 1840
Newgate Prison, London

At last my husband put pen assuredly to paper, his fanciful infatuation with the Queen faded and his good humour, for a time, restored.

He stood in front of the hall mirror, tying his cravat and whistling cheerfully, He was dressed in a sober fashion, which was for him unusual, and was wearing a black armband. Not being aware of the death of any of our acquaintances, I was puzzled.

'Has someone who we know died, dear?'

'No, no one we know.' He was humming to himself now.

'Then one of your colleagues?'

'No, not one of my colleagues,' he responded unhelpfully, and continued to hum.

'Then where are you going?' I persisted.

He hesitated for a moment, unsure whether to satisfy my curiosity, then he smoothed down his hair, reached for his hat from the hat stand and replied, 'I am going, my dear, to a hanging.'

'A hanging!' I was shocked at such an idea. 'Whatever for?'

I was aware that Charles had been caught up in the trial of Courvoisier, the Swiss-born valet who had murdered his elderly master, but to go to the gates of Newgate Prison and witness such a vile spectacle as his death, how could Charles do such a thing?

'A little bit of research,' he said, with a ghoulish voice, attempting to be amusing. A sharp rap at the door caused me to jump. Talk of such a macabre subject had unnerved me.

I was surprised to see William Thackeray on the doorstep and to find that he too was attired in a cheerless manner.

'Good morning, my dear William!' Charles chirped, shaking his friend's hand in an enthusiastic welcome. William greeted me with a somewhat diffident smile and seemed unusually awkward and uneasy in my presence. I pondered for a moment over his appearance and hesitant manner, then all at once I understood.

'Oh, William! Not you too?'

Charles came to his defence. 'Kate, a writer must stay abreast of what is happening, if he is to write with any conviction, isn't that so, William?'

William didn't know which way to move his head, not wanting to disagree with his dear friend, whom he greatly admired, nor to offend my female sensibility. Charles snatched up his cane, put on his hat with a tap and grimaced theatrically. We shall see you later, Kate!'

The newspapers had been filled with reports about the sensational trial. The victim was Lord William Russell, brother to the Duke of Bedford, and the court had been crowded by those eager to learn more about his bloody end. François Benjamin Courvoisier had taken a knife to his master's throat while he slept in his bed and then made it appear as though a robbery had taken place during the night. The housemaid had found the lower floor in a state of disturbance the following morning, and had scurried in various directions calling for the cook and valet to come to her aid. The furniture was upturned, the cupboards and drawers opened and emptied. It was then that a terrible thought had entered her mind: 'What of his lordship?' She and Courvoisier had gone upstairs and found the aged gentleman, dead, his pillow soaked with blood. The poor girl had screamed and shouted for the neighbours to come to their aid.

The paper reported that, despite the valet showing the police where the thieves had purportedly entered the premises, he found difficulty answering their other questions. When a search of the premises had been made, many articles of his lordship's were found under the floorboards in Courvoisier's room and under his mattress: a gold watch, a silver toothpick, a locket bearing a lock of hair belonging to his lordship's departed wife, and a good deal of gold and silver coin too.

Courvoisier changed his story repeatedly, first blaming the housemaid and then the coachman, with whom he said the maid was in love and wished to elope. Mr Edward Flower, an experienced attorney, was employed to conduct the defence as a result of the large subscription that had been raised by the many foreign servants in London, who wanted to see the valet receive a fair trial. At first Courvoisier had been confident, almost defiant, but when the landlady of a French hotel in Leicester Square came forward with some silver candlesticks – passed to her by the defendant some weeks before Lord Russell's murder – he confessed all. The jury found him guilty and Lord Chief Justice Tindal sentenced Courvoisier to death by hanging.

In the early hours of the morning Charles returned home. I heard him groaning and went at once to the top of the stairs, sensing that his buoyant mood of earlier had disappeared. He was slumped on the bottom step, his head in his hands.

'Charles what has happened? Are you unwell?'

I hurried down the stairs, crouched down beside him and lifting his face, saw that his complexion was waxen – and I was suddenly repulsed by the smell of vomit upon his clothing. He groaned again.

'It was a night with the demons, Kate, I wish that I had not witnessed it. The surging crowd were filthy and immoral, I had to rent a room with a balcony just to avoid my pockets being picked. Even the women were drunk and hurled about obscenities while jostling for a place at the front. I cannot conceive that my fellow humans could act with such barbarity.' He shuddered. 'Do you know that they cheered when the body swung?' At this he rested his head on my shoulder in distress at the memory.

I shivered as the image passed before my eyes and I was lost for words to comfort him. I laid my hand upon his head and stroked his hair with sympathetic tenderness, grateful of his need for me, if only for the moment. Two days later, Charles wrote to *The Times* and made public his outrage at the degraded practice, stating that the law was as guilty as the criminal in carrying out such a punishment. And thus he began the campaign for the abolition of the death penalty.

CHAPTER EIGHTEEN

August 1840
Broadstairs, Kent

Another summer was spent at Broadstairs. The morning
newspaper lay unread on the breakfast table; a review of *The Old
Curiosity Shop* was contained within and Charles feared that his
eye might chance upon it while perusing the columns. He need
not have worried: although *Master Humphrey's Clock* had left his
readers feeling disappointed at its brevity, he had quickly set to
work on *The Old Curiosity Shop* and had judged the mood of his
audience with exactitude.

Unaware of his success, he was in a restless mood. Upon
arrival at the holiday cottage he first satisfied himself that the
sleeping arrangements were in all order, next he had rearranged
the sitting-room furniture, moving one chair, then another, until
it pleased him. Finally he took out all of the crockery and began
to count the plates.

'You never know, Kate, we are sure to have visitors.'

I begged him to come and relax in the garden, but instead he
whipped up the children into a frenzy by chasing them about,
roaring and growling, and the air was punctuated with the
squeals of childish delight. Eventually, worn out, he sat down.
He tried out several places on the lawn, but got up repeatedly to
remove a twig or to stamp down a bump in the soil. At last he

settled, lay down and put a handkerchief over his face. A few seconds and in time the handkerchief was drawn in and out with each gentle breath that he took.

Then in one bound, he leapt to his feet and charged into the cottage!

'Heaven preserve us what is he doing now?' I sighed.

Ten minutes later he emerged with an envelope in his hand and declared with satisfaction that he had invited guests to join us. Was it really so impossible for him to spend even a few days alone with just his family?

Mr and Mrs Charles Smithson, their niece Eleanor Picken and her friend Millicent Brown, arrived at the end of the week and they brought with them sunny skies. Mr Smithson grasped Charles's hand with such zeal I thought he would fall down on his knees in an act of worship.

'Mr Dickens! Mr Dickens! What a pleasure to see you again.'

His niece, Eleanor, was a slim, attractive girl with golden blonde hair that was ringleted in the latest fashion about her face. She was equally in awe of meeting Charles, but I watched as she very carefully appraised his appearance and noted how her face changed to one of disappointment as she took in his small stature and gaudy waistcoat. Her demeanour alternated frequently between insincere sweetness and subtle spite, with her poor companion Millie usually on the receiving end.

Millie spoke very quickly, blushed easily and always seemed to be tripping over something; here I sympathized with her, being naturally unsteady upon my own feet. She was a slightly built girl who looked no more than fourteen, although she must have been nearly twenty, and the wire glasses which rested on a homely nose, did nothing to enhance her plain features.

Eleanor inspected the cottage with an air of dissatisfaction and wrinkled up her pretty nose with distaste. 'Had I known that Mr Dickens was holidaying in a fisherman's cottage, I would have instructed Uncle to take private rooms elsewhere, Millie.' She then set about ordering her friend to unpack her bags, hang up her clothes and to close the windows for she could not stand the smell of the sea air.

I had not met Mr Smithson before, but learned that my husband had met the solicitor through his old colleague, Thomas Mitten, a former clerk at the courts where Charles had worked as a reporter. Mitten now worked in Mr Smithson's chambers and had made the introduction when his employer expressed enjoyment of my husband's work. Mr Smithson was a portly man with huge whiskers and several chins, and his spouse was equally stout. It was whispered that before they had moved to the City that she had at one time been his cook and that he had married her after the death of his first wife. If this were true, proof of her culinary talents were still in evidence: a button was missing from his tightly fitted waistcoat and those that remained were straining to retain their hold upon the material.

'Pleased to make your h'aquintance, Mrs Dickens.' Mrs Smithson curtsied unnecessarily, trying to adopt the airs and graces she felt were required by her new-found station in life. I took in her dress, which was patterned all over with large flowers and adorned with needless frippery and finery upon her sleeves, cuffs and collar. To my mind, a stout woman should never wear rosettes and ribbons, for they call to attention every pound of flesh a lady should want to minimize. If good taste was any indication of good sense, then I could see that a holiday spent with Mrs Smithson was not one to be relished.

Charles was to be thanked for providing all the entertainment we needed. In the evenings he organized guessing games, dancing, or walks along the beach, and when Daniel Maclise, the artist, joined us the following week, he delighted us with his clever sketches of passers-by. One evening, while walking along the beach, a look of mischief crossed my husband's face and, without warning, he dashed towards Eleanor, falling down upon one knee before her feet.

'Dearest Ellie' – he took her gloved hand – 'please say that you will treasure these few brief moments we have spent together, and never forsake me!'

Eleanor looked about her with embarrassment, and then her face formed a scowl of disapproval. 'Please do not jest so, Mr Dickens. Get up! Get up! People are watching.'

'I care not!' he exclaimed dramatically, clasping her hand to his heart, 'What are the opinions of others to me when I am bewitched by your very presence?'

A small audience had now gathered and Millie giggled with delight, glad for once to see her friend feeling awkward and embarrassed.

'Mrs Dickens, please will you call your husband off!' A note of hysteria had entered into Eleanor's voice.

I, too, delighted in the spectacle, but tried my best to comply with her request.

'Charles, come now, the young lady has had enough.'

'Enough? I have not yet even begun.' At which he scooped her up in his arms and ran along the beach with her until he reached the water's edge.

Mrs Smithson forgot her propriety and squealed, 'Lord, luv-a-duck! 'E's goin' to soak 'er!' She caught the astonished glance of her husband and submitted, 'I meant to say, her dress is silk, sir.'

'Talk not to me of silk, madam,' Charles shouted, dancing in the waves, 'I am a man possessed! This is no time for prudence.'

By now Millie was pressing her handkerchief to her mouth in an effort to disguise her mirth at the sight of Eleanor kicking her legs and thrashing her arms about.

'Uncle! Will you tell him to loose me at once.'

'Come now, Dickens,' Smithson cajoled, 'put her down – there's a good fellow.'

Charles stopped in his tracks, looked at Eleanor and, with the words, "it seems, my dear, that we are destined to be parted", he dropped her into the water. When Eleanor surfaced, her curls in disarray, she screamed with rage. She fixed a malevolent glare upon Charles, slapped her uncle on the arm as he tried to escort her, and ordered Millie to her side at once, beginning an indignant retreat to the cottage.

'The man's a madman! That's what Charles Dickens is – a complete madman!'

CHAPTER NINETEEN

May 1841
Kensal Green Cemetery, London

'Are you not hungry this morning, madam?' Emily asked, hovering in the doorway of my bedroom, with uncertainty.

I lay staring at the ceiling above, concentrating on the lines and curves of the coving until they blurred into one. Two triangles of toast, a hard boiled egg and a cup of milky tea sat untouched on a silver tray at my bedside. It was the fourth anniversary of Mary's death and I earnestly wished that I could put off my visit to the cemetery. I couldn't imagine anything that would be able to pass beyond the persistent ache in my throat.

'Thank you, Emily, but I'm not in the least bit hungry. Can you take it away, please, and bring me a cup of lemon tea instead?'

I got out of bed and opened the window to let in the morning air. The day was bright, a pleasant breeze brushing through the trees. The street below carried the reassuring sounds that life outside these four walls was carrying on as normal: the squeaking wheels of the chimney-sweep's cart, the hurried footsteps of a maid, two ladies each admiring the other's hat.

Charles had already left for the City. He said that he would not be going with me to the cemetery as he had an appointment with his publishers. I experienced a mixture of surprise and relief at his words – perhaps at last his ongoing obsession with my sister was over. We never spoke of her now and he continued to hide behind the same detached façade, so who could begin to know what he felt? But his actions that morning had given me some hope.

A black crepe dress lay across the bed. For three long months after Mary's death I had done my duty and dressed in mourning. It was a terrible burden, a daily reminder that she had gone forever. Whatever small joy that could have been found was extinguished with the putting on of those sombre vestments. It was such a relief when that obligation was over, but today I had to return to it again. I picked up the dress and a swirl of images flooded my mind: Charles cradling Mary in his arms and calling her name, the doctor shaking his head and trying to part Charles from her lifeless body, the sense of despair that had filled the room.

Emily returned with the tea and set a jug of hot water on the washstand but I have no recollection of washing, for I was lost in thought, wondering how life would have been if Mary were still here, questioning if Charles's life with me would have been more satisfying to him – her wit and zest for life bringing to our home what I could not seem to.

Emily laced me into the dress and I held onto the back of a chair feeling light-headed.

'Are you sure you are all right, madam? Shall I call the doctor?'

'Please don't fuss, Emily, I am fine. Mrs Thackeray will be here soon, I must finish dressing.'

Isabella had kindly offered to accompany me to the cemetery, and I was grateful for her support. When the doorbell rang to announce her arrival, I pinched my cheeks, trying to bring some colour to my pallid complexion and came downstairs with a brave smile. But Isabella was not fooled at all.

'Perhaps it is best if you do not stay out too long,' she said with concern, examining my face closely.

'I do wish everybody would stop treating me like an invalid,' I snapped, and then immediately regretted my hastiness.

Isabella graciously ignored my irritation and we stepped into the waiting carriage. The weather was good which helped soothe my troubled nerves and gave Isabella and I something meaningless to talk about. Leaving the fringes of the City I caught sight of children, both ragged and forlorn and I pitied their unhappy existence. I realized, once again, that I was blessed. My children had a good home, clean beds to sleep in and nourishing food each day.

Eventually the gates to the cemetery came into sight and Isabella squeezed my hand, sensing how I felt.

'Shall I come with you?' she asked gently.

'No, thank you, Izzy. I would prefer to be alone.'

I stepped down from the carriage and followed the gravel path that cut across grassy, uneven ground.

As I moved the overhanging branches of an oak tree near the end of the path, I saw a familiar figure crouched at Mary's graveside. His brown wavy hair blew about gently in the breeze and his brightly coloured waistcoat stood out amidst the scattered grey headstones. I could see his lips moving and every so often he would stop and break into an anguished sob. I was gripped by a sudden nausea and ducked back behind the branches of the tree, leaning against its rough grained trunk for a moment. When I had regained my composure I checked again to make sure of what I had seen. Charles was still crouched down and had now grasped a handful of gravel from the grave. He was holding it to his lips, his fist clenched tightly around it. He let it go and then reached out his hand, tracing the letters of Mary's name with his forefinger. His hand trembled and, as his finger finished the final letter, he put his hands to his face and became broken with grief, his shoulders heaving with despair.

I turned and began to run, struggling in my pregnant state. *He said he wasn't going; he said he would be too busy. Why did he lie? Why did he lie?* The thoughts circled round and round in my mind and I stumbled back to the coach, choking on my tears.

'Was it really too much for you, dear Kate?' Isabella said, as she opened the coach door, helping me in.

I could not reveal the true cause of my distress and nodded, taking a handkerchief from my purse. Isabella motioned to the perplexed driver to move on, and tried to calm me down. When the carriage drew up outside Devonshire Terrace, I hesitated, not wanting to get out. What reason did I have to be wife to a man for whom I was so obviously second choice?

Misjudging the reason for my uncertainty, Isabella placed her hand upon mine and said:

'Shall I call for Charles to come home to you?'

'No, please!' I said with alarm, and then with mock composure, 'I will be fine, really. Thank you, Izzy, you have already been so kind.'

I wished that the driver of that carriage would pull away with me inside and keep driving, but I remembered my children: Charley, serious and shy, Mary gentle as a lamb, Katie restless and bright-eyed and baby Walter. With a deep sigh I squeezed Isabella's hand, stepped down from the carriage and crossed over the threshold of Devonshire Terrace once more.

It was late, I lay in bed, waiting for him to return, feeling that there was so much that I wanted to say. I recognized his quick-footed gait upon the footpath below and heard the front door open. I hoped that he would not take to his study tonight for I could hold my tongue no longer and I did not want to go downstairs and speak to him in the hearing of the servants. The bedroom door opened and a look of surprise crossed my husband's face.

'Oh, I did not expect you to still be awake, my dear, it's late.'

He went to the wash stand, splashed his face and towelled himself dry. I harnessed courage, sat up and began quietly, 'I saw you today.'

'Kate,' he sighed, 'would you please make your meaning clear. I am tired and not at all interested in guessing games.'

'I saw you at the cemetery. At Mary's graveside. You said that you would not be going.' My voice wavered.

'I said that I would not be going with *you*.' he replied, pulling his shirt over his head. 'That is not the same thing at all.'

He threw the covers back, climbed into bed and turned on his side. But I was not about to give up.

'I know why you lied, Charles, why you didn't want me there with you. You feared that I would guess the truth, didn't you? The truth about how you really felt about Mary.' My heart hammered on my chest. 'Why don't you be honest with me? Why don't you tell me that it was my sister that you loved all along?'

He punched at his pillow and sat upright. 'For the love of God, woman! My feelings for Mary are something that you could never understand in a lifetime. They have become something impure in your mind, something twisted and polluted by your jealousy. *That* is the reason that I did not go to the cemetery with you, and that reason alone.'

He swung his legs out of bed, reached for his shirt and began dressing himself angrily.

Was it true? Were my old insecurities clouding my judgement again?

'But where are you going?'

'Now, i am too cross to sleep. Now I have to go out again and calm myself down!'

'Charles! Please, I just—'

But he left the room with a bang of the door and I sat alone in the candlelight, wondering which one of us it was had been in the wrong after all.

CHAPTER TWENTY

June 1841
Edinburgh, Scotland

The incident at the graveside was not mentioned again, and Charles continued to be cordial in all his dealings with me and so I realized that some things were best left unspoken.

At the repeated invitation of Lord Jeffrey, Charles agreed to pay a visit to Edinburgh and asked me to accompany him. Not usually an enthusiastic traveller, on this occasion, however, I was keen to go. I thought Edinburgh was a beautiful city and it was especially close to my heart, being the place of my birth.

Upon our arrival at The Royal Hotel we were informed that Lord Jeffrey was unwell and that he had nominated Sir George Robertson to act as our escort and guide in his stead. The elderly judge was a great admirer of my husband's work and welcomed him with the words, 'Ye've the mind of a genius, young sir, there's no doubt about it. And all of Edinburgh will be there tonight to welcome ye.'

Our rooms were splendid and Charles declared that he would have our bedroom at home painted the same delicate pink that adorned the walls of our suite. Sir George had talked of there being 300 at dinner and I felt a great sense of unease at the thought of it. Charles shone brilliantly on such occasions, but I preferred to stay in the background knowing that I did not sparkle in the way of great beauty or wit at all. As eight o' clock approached, the uneasiness had moved to my stomach and I felt so sure that I would pass out at the dinner table that I begged to be excused. Charles looked greatly displeased, asking why I had not said something sooner.

'Now you have made me nervous too!' he snapped, struggling to button his collar.

We were driven to the Halls of the Courts of Law and arrived to a rapturous reception. Sir George introduced us to all the waiting dignitaries and I thought that he was going to burst with the pride of doing so. Sometimes I really marvelled at the spell which my husband seemed to cast over people. At dinner I was seated next to Sir George's wife and was surprised to note that although the elderly lady had a glass of soda water in front of her, she did not touch it at all, preferring instead to take an occasional sip of whisky from a hip flask hidden in her bag.

Over the days that followed we toured the length and breadth of the city. Its architecture was breathtaking and Charles wanted to see it all. Lord Jeffrey recovered his spirits and was keen to accompany us to Princes Street where we admired the Greek inspired Royal Institution, along with Register House and its magnificent central dome designed by Robert Adam. In Charlotte Square we inspected Bute House and marvelled at its many decorative sash windows and palace-like façade. Looking up through the eternally spiralling staircase in the grand hall, I felt quite giddy!

Although the early days of our holiday had been an exhausting round of breakfasts, banquets and tours of the city I endured them all with one clear goal in mind: to visit the house where I had been born. I had often dreamt of being there again, imagining I had returned to my childhood, but to see it once more in reality filled me with great excitement and now at last the opportunity had presented itself. Charles, however – to my great disappointment – was reluctant to accompany me.

'I am tired out, Kate. Besides, a man has no interest in plate, silver or linen. I have a chapter to finish and dispatch, I really do not have the time.'

But I begged him, saying that as I had accompanied him all around Edinburgh surely he could do the one thing that I desired most. He looked upon me sternly and then consulted his watch.

'One hour, Kate, and no longer. You really must not put me under obligation you know.'

I thanked him earnestly and promised that I would be quiet on the journey should he wish to work.

When the coach turned into the driveway, I peered intently out of the window to catch the first glimpse of my childhood home. I was filled with delight when I saw that the front of the house had not changed at all, except for the two large conifers either side of the front door, which must have been planted not long after my family moved. There was also a cobbled courtyard leading to a newly built coach house at the back. At one time this had been a vegetable patch where the gardener had wheeled his barrowful of greens across to the kitchen window.

We knocked at the door and waited a few minutes without any reply. Charles took out his watch again and sighed before returning it to his waistcoat pocket.

'There is no one here, Kate, we might as well go.'

I was just about to knock once more when the door was opened by a rather dour butler. He looked as though we had awoken him from a very deep sleep and that he was quite put out about it. We learned that the owners were abroad and that the house was unoccupied, but when my husband introduced himself as Mr Charles Dickens the butler's manner changed completely and he welcomed us in with great haste.

The hallway echoed with our footsteps and I noticed through a half open door that the old kitchen had gone and a morning room was in its place.

'The kitchen is now in the basement, madam,' the butler said, reading my thoughts.

I knew my mother would have approved of that, having never liked the smells that sometimes crept into the rest of the house.

'May I see it?' I enquired.

He nodded and motioned that I should follow him. Charles, however, had lost interest already but had noticed a bookcase in the study to which he was immediately drawn.

I made my way down a stone staircase to the basement. A large pine table dominated the room, blanched pale through scrubbing. The range was unlit and consequently the room was dark and chilly, and I noticed the cobwebs in the corners of the adjoining scullery and judged that there was no housekeeper here at present. I remembered the irascible cook who had worked for my parents, her hands red raw from work, her large bunch of keys jangling at her waist. There was little chance of any food escaping unnoticed from her larder! I could almost hear the crisp crackle of roasting chicken on the spit and her stern words not to get too close to the range. But this lifeless space showed little signs of activity other than a spinning spider in the scullery and with no cook to offer hospitality or a recipe tip, I followed the butler back into the main house where I found Charles engrossed in a book.

'Charles, why don't you come and see the nursery where Mary and I used to sleep?'

Grudgingly he put down the novel and accompanied me and, as I held the banister to go up the stairs, an image flitted across my mind: I was a child again, peering through the spindles and watching Mama and Papa leave for the theatre. I heard the imagined echo of their voices, *'George! We are going to be late.'*

'Hush, my dear, we will make it in good time, don't worry, now.'

And I smiled at the memory.

We continued up the stairs and at the end of the landing opened the door to what had once been my bedroom. The curtains billowed from an open window into an empty room and the butler crossed the room to close it. There was neither crib nor toys and I shivered, suddenly filled with an overwhelming sadness: an image of Mary crawling across the nursery floor had come unbidden into my mind and I expelled it with a sigh.

'Are you all right, Kate?' Charles asked with uncustomary concern.

'Just unexpected memories, that is all,' I replied, as the nursery door was closed.

Feeling now more sadness than joy, I walked around the remainder of the house disengaged, lost in thought; visiting the house had fulfilled a wish that I had long held, but it had been a mistake. I would not come back again.

Driving away, Charles picked up the morning newspaper and returned to something that had caught his eye earlier.

'Look at this, Kate!' he enthused prodding the open pages of the *Morning Chronicle*. 'Coach and two horses for sale – forty guineas. If it's as good as it sounds then we'd have no more need of hiring a carriage. What do you say?'

Having very little interest in any moving vehicle, I nodded and smiled, feigning interest. He directed the driver to a nearby farm.

'We'll go and have a look, Kate, eh? Might as well while we're in the area.'

It had grown dark.

'Where on earth are we?'

Charles strained his eyes to look out into the night. The darkness was foreboding. 'What is this terrible place?'

Over the last few days we had left Edinburgh, and travelled on to Stirling and Melrose, and were now on the Glencoe Pass.

The carriage creaked and moved from side to side, jolting me repeatedly against an angry and frightened husband. The windows did not provide a water-tight barrier between the storm and ourselves and the driving rain found an opening, its icy fingers darting into the coach and gradually dampening us. The visit to the farm had been a waste of time; the coach and horses had not been worth forty guineas at all and the farmer would not budge on his price.

A flash of lightning illuminated the carriage, transforming Charles and myself into ghostly images. Charles banged on the roof and called to the driver.

'How much further?'

If the driver replied his voice was carried away by the wind and for a terrifying moment I imagined an unmanned coach driven by two possessed horses heading for Hades. When the lightning flashed once more I saw that we were on the Glencoe Pass on a steep decline, and that the bridge across the river was flooded.

I clutched at my husband's arm. 'Charles, I'm frightened.'

The carriage was swaying violently now and seemed to be gaining speed. Suddenly the driver made his presence known shouting, 'Sir! Madam! You must jump out! We are heading for the river!'

I was paralysed with fear and could not move.

'Kate, you heard him, we have to get out.' Charles threw open the carriage door and held out his hand, but, as the coach hit a hard place in the road he was hurled through the open door, leaving me behind. The driver leapt clear too and the carriage hurtled uncontrollably into the swollen river. With incredible bravery the man dived into the moving waters and managed to pull me free. One of the horses struggled to loose itself from the harness and succeeded, but the other poor creature was pulled away to its death. Charles staggered to his feet and waded part way into the water to help. His hair was caked with mud, and streaks of blood washed onto his face with the rain. Back on dry land I was lifted onto the remaining horse and that dear lame animal limped through the darkness until we found shelter in a remote inn.

Charles pressed several coins into the driver's shaking hand and thanked him profusely. The man tugged his forelock and sat down to drain a large tumbler of whisky. The innkeeper's wife wrapped us up in blankets and we sat and stared into the fire trying to expel from our minds the image of the carriage turning over and over. The other patrons attempted to disguise their furtive glances and in the low hum of chatter we heard the words, 'Dickens ... almost killed ... his poor wife nearly drowned. . . .'

When we had warmed through sufficiently to go to bed,

neither of us could sleep, being woken with a frightening start each time our eyelids finally closed. Charles held on to me tightly and cried intermittently.

'Kate, I was so frightened… I thought that I had lost you forever . . . if I. . . .' He choked on his words and then tried again. 'If I ever seem…that is, if I sometimes struggle to express how I feel about you know now that I care more than I can say, almost losing you has made me realize that.'

In spite of the day's events, I felt a strange sense of peace: a woman can exist a long time on the memory of such words.

CHAPTER TWENTY-ONE

November 1841
Devonshire Terrace

It was a dull morning: a dense cover of grey, without sign of where each cloud began and ended. I sat in the drawing room, struggling to sew in the poor light. I was trying to alter the children's clothes; they were growing up so quickly. Charles would remind me again and again that he was a man of means now and that there was really no need for me to make do, but it gave me a meaningful way to spend my time, and losing myself in the rhythmic cycle of the needle was soothing when my old anxieties returned.

I heard my husband's striding gait across the hallway and waited for the turn of the door knob which I knew would follow. The door flew open with the words:

'Ah, there you are, Kate! Kate, I have decided: I want you to accompany me on a trip to America, I can't do without you for any great length of time and there is no point in my going for a short trip, so you must come with me.'

He dropped into the chair opposite me, as if the speech had momentarily taken all the life out of him. A second later his foot was tapping impatiently, willing me to hurry up and make a decision.

'But Charles, I don't think the children would be up to such a strenuous tour, they're still so little.'

He dropped his eyes to the floor and brushed an imaginary speck from his trousers. Putting my sewing aside I leaned forward earnestly.

'Charles, you can't begin to think of asking me to leave them, and how could you yourself bear to leave them for so long?'

He got up from the chair and turned away, not wanting me to see his face. Although he mastered his emotions well enough in front of others, I knew him too intimately to be fooled.

'Well?' I persisted.

He cleared his throat. 'The children will be fine. I have asked Macready and his wife to see to them and they are quite willing.'

He strolled about the room straightening a chair, the tablecloth, a protruding book on the shelf; arranging everything around him as he was now arranging my life, as if he knew that I would protest no more than those inanimate objects to being moved about where I might not want to go.

I picked up my sewing again with a decisive action.

'Well, I shall not leave them, even if you can,' I said petulantly.

Charles spun around suddenly, his eyes blazing. 'I do not think you understand me, my dear. I have said that I cannot do without you and I that want you to come with me. Now I have made all the arrangements and everything is set, so please do not upset me with one of your moods. We will not be leaving for a month, so you will have plenty of time to sort out your wardrobe and say goodbye to the children.'

He turned to leave, desperate to avoid further discussion and, with a swift bang, closed the door behind him.

'Sort out my wardrobe and say goodbye to the children.' As if one could be as easily done as the other! I paced about the room, seeing their little faces, imagining them crying, thinking about not seeing them for months, maybe never seeing them again if we were lost at sea.

'No! I can't leave them. He shouldn't ask me to.'

I grasped at the curtains, burying my face, finding comfort in their softness like a child seeking refuge in her mother's skirts. Why couldn't he let me stay? He could take Forster, or one of his other acquaintances. Why me? Yet how often had I anguished over the times when he had seemed cold and distant, appearing to prefer everyone else's company above mine. Now here at last he was asking for my companionship and my support on this adventure. If I refused to go, he might never forgive me. And how could I ever rightly complain of his neglect again? If only I did not have to choose my duty as a wife above my devotion as a mother. But maybe the children were more resilient than I knew. Perhaps they would enjoy their stay with the Macreadys.

I moved over to the desk and sat down. I thought for a moment and then began to write. It was not a list of the things that I would need for the trip, but of the things that my children needed:

Don't overexcite Charley at bedtime – he has bad dreams.
And Mary, she has a favourite toy that she likes to sleep with.
Katie – she prefers to sleep on her front.
And Baby Walter, he finds it soothing if you sing to him at night. . . .

January 1842
Liverpool

I was exhausted by the stressful morning, making sure that we had everything and then journeying to Liverpool. Charles, confined by the coach, had nearly driven me mad with his restless fidgeting. I was wearing a blue velvet travelling suit with matching hat and muff. Charles wore a charcoal, full-length greatcoat with a large fur collar, his bright red cravat peeking above at the neck. It had taken him the best part of one day to pack his trunk. He had refused all offers of help and had rearranged the items within over and over until he was satisfied.

We stood now at the docks: myself, Charles, his sister Fanny, her husband Albert, and Forster. Charles could not stand still for a moment. He had already gone to check on the luggage several times, firstly to make sure that it was all there – two large trunks, one smaller trunk and two carpet-bags – then, as soon as he returned to us he threw his hands in the air as if remembering something else and went back to check that the locks were secure.

'My papers are in that small trunk, Kate. They must not be disturbed,' he called over his shoulder as he disappeared.

When he wanted to make sure that the porter had remembered to be careful with the carpet-bags because they could easily be squashed, I sighed with exasperation. 'Charles you cannot disturb that poor man again.'

Forster announced, 'Leave this to me, madam, I will come to your husband's aid.'

Fanny was no comfort to me either. Knowing how unstable her brother's mood was, she directed her fussing and flapping at me instead.

'Now have you packed suitable clothes, Sister? Plenty of warm petticoats. The weather will be quite bitter there now.'

'Yes, Fanny. I have what I need!' I hissed, not wanting my undergarments discussed for all to hear.

'And have you put in some of your larger sized dresses? You will be attending a lot of dinners, and you know how you are inclined to put on weight easily.'

Albert shuffled with unease at his wife's tactlessness, but I chose to ignore her comment for fear of losing my temper once and for all. Charles took out his comb and gave his hair a ritualistic tidy. Then he fetched out his watch and frowned.

'I wonder what's happened to Forster, he's been gone ages. I must go and find him.'

Fanny opened her mouth again as if to speak again and so I pleaded, 'No, Charles, let *me* go; I need to stretch my legs,' and broke away quickly before he could object.

I spotted Forster's tall silhouette moving toward me amid the heaving crowds. The ship's horn blew and a cloud of steam descended, obliterating him from sight for a moment. Mindful that it was time to start boarding, I was grateful to see him reappear through the swirling steam.

'There you are, John. Charles thought that you had got lost.'

He took my arm and said. 'You will help to keep him calm while he's away, won't you, Catherine? He has many things on his mind, especially his campaign to gain a copyright agreement between England and America. I have secured his interests here, but I will not be there to help him on the other side of the water, you know. I worry that he will over-exert himself.'

I was touched by Forster's concern. Despite his pompous nature, I could not fault the sincerity of his friendship with my husband.

'I cannot promise to bring any influence to bear on my husband's temperament. As you know only too well, John, Charles is not directed by anything other than his own will. But I will try.'

As we returned to the others, Charles hurried toward us, gesturing at the ship.

'We must get aboard now, my dear. Please don't delay.'

Forster shook Charles heartily by the hand and gave him a small package. Charles unwrapped it and took out a pocket book of Shakespeare. He embraced his friend and said, 'How foolish I was ever to have quarrelled with you in the past, my dear Forster. I will keep this with me throughout my trip and remember that I have a brother waiting at home for my return.'

We stepped onto the boarding plank and once aboard, jostled for a position on the deck, looking for familiar faces on dry land. When the ship set sail at last, we stood and waved until Forster, Fanny and Albert were insignificant dots on the quay.

CHAPTER TWENTY-TWO

January 1842
The Britannia

Plagued by terrible toothache, Charles rubbed his jaw.

'This cabin is no larger than a matchbox.' He groaned. 'And the windows are nailed shut. How am I supposed to breathe?'

He banged the porthole again violently in the hope that it might finally give way.

'Dear God, Kate, I am sick of this leaky vessel! It has only been two days since we left home and already I long to be on dry land.'

He lay down on the bunk and wriggled, trying to get comfortable, before complaining again. 'This ship feels as though it will capsize at any moment, there are no lifeboats and if the deck doesn't catch fire from the sparking funnel it will be a miracle!'

At another surge of pain in his tooth he sat up suddenly, banging his head on the bunk above. He leapt off the bed and hopped from one foot to the other, holding his head and shouting things which I cannot write down here. My own head throbbed, I felt sick and dizzy and Charles's temper was doing nothing to bring me relief. I struggled to think how I might help him. What would Forster do if he were here? I thought about Forster, his irritating voice and embellished story-telling. Charles would revel in his companionship and banter; I, however, could not provide that but perhaps I could find someone who might.

There were eighty-five passengers aboard this boat and everyone of them would no doubt relish the privilege of meeting the 'inimitable' Charles Dickens. There had to be at least one among them who could distract my irritable husband with stimulating company. When Charles had settled himself on the bed again, I left the cabin in search of someone with sufficient character to capture my husband's interest.

I mingled amidst the varied passengers: the toothless and pipe smoking, the cultivated and wealthy. I heard a hearty laugh and saw near the brow of the ship a tall, distinctive figure. I could not see his face, but standing at more than six feet tall his physical bearing carried a strong sense of authority. At his side was a petite, exquisitely dressed woman who was holding onto his arm with great affection. They turned so that I could see their faces and continued their animated conversation. He had a large bristly beard, peppered with red, that matched his auburn curly hair. His eyes sparkled with mischief and, when he laughed, it was with such resonance that he caused passers-by to turn and smile. His tiny wife was dark-haired, perhaps little more than twenty. She caught my glance and smiled, revealing a set of beautiful white teeth. I returned her smile and felt a little embarrassed at having been caught watching them. But I remembered my mission and found the courage to approach them.

I held out my hand in greeting. 'May I introduce myself? I am Mrs Catherine Dickens. I'm sorry if I appeared to be staring but I was quite struck by your charming outfit, madam.'

The lady held out her hand in return and said, 'Thank you, Mrs Dickens, I purchased it in Spain.' Her voice revealed an accent that undoubtedly came from the same location.

'My name is Consuela Swift and this is my husband, Doctor Thomas Swift.'

'Pleased to meet you, ma'am.' He enthused, grasping my hand so hard that I thought it would break.

'Are you a doctor of medicine, sir? For if you are, then you might be able to bring some relief to my poor husband.'

'I would be glad to help, Mrs Dickens. Lead the way.'

I gestured in the direction of our cabin and used the short walk to reveal the identity of my husband and to explain how our confined quarters and seasickness were not being improved by his terrible toothache. I tapped nervously on the door of the cabin. 'Charles, I have brought someone to see you.'

He groaned in response. 'Kate, I am hardly in any mood for company. Tell them to come back later.'

'But it is a doctor, Charles. He might be able to help you.'

A few moments of silence were followed by the rustling of clothes being hastily donned and the click of the cabin door opening. Pale-faced, Charles peered through the crack in the door. His hair was in wild disarray, having been underneath an ice-bag.

'Good-day to you, sir, I am Dr Thomas Swift. If the ladies will excuse us, I hope that you will permit me to come to your aid.'

A sense of relief washed over Charles's face and he stood aside meekly, allowing the giant of a man to enter the cabin. I turned to Mrs Swift, 'And perhaps, madam, you can tell me more about that outfit of yours.'

It took fifteen days to cross that turbulent ocean and the difficult journey was only endured because of our new-found friendship with the Swifts. Thomas was everything that my first impressions had conveyed, warm-hearted, with a jovial disposition that endeared him to all who met him. His intellect and humour were the best medicine that Charles could have taken on that unsteady crossing. I discovered that Thomas and his wife were emigrating to America so that he could take up the directorship of The Institute for the Deaf in Philadelphia. Thomas believed in social reform for the less privileged and, like Charles, believed that America was leading the way in this area. He and Consuela had met in Madrid. Her father was a diplomat and had taken some persuading to let his youngest daughter marry, but had eventually been won over by Thomas's charm and reassurances that he would guard Consuela with his own life. They had been wed less than six months and were now about to embark on a new life across the water.

Despite her diminutive size, Consuela mirrored her husband's enthusiasm for life and it did not take long before Charles displayed signs of being completely besotted with her. He would spend longer than usual combing his hair and tying his cravat, but I tried not to be too dismayed and hoped that this would just be one of his passing infatuations. However, I could not help but feel outshone: envious of her tiny figure and dazzling wardrobe. It was not only my physical shortcomings that I was reminded of. Over dinner it became evident that in addition to speaking English, Consuela was fluent in Italian and French also. Charles joked about my own achievements.

'I suspect that you did not know that my wife is also an author?' he said with a twinkle in his eye.

Thomas and Consuela looked at me with interest and surprise, and I began to panic.

'It was only a little cookery book,' I admitted, my face reddening with embarrassment.

There was a moment's silence and then Charles turned to Consuela and asked about her father's distinguished career. I watched as he listened intently, seemingly mesmerized by her moving lips. Thomas kindly asked me about the children and for a moment I felt at ease talking about that which was closest to my heart.

At the sound of the accordion playing a reel, Charles jumped up and grasped Consuela's hand, 'You don't mind if I borrow your wife, do you, Thomas?'

Thomas nodded his consent, apparently taking Charles's interest in his wife as a great compliment.

When the boat docked at Boston, a bitter frost and sharp wind bit deep into our bodies. What hopes we had had of a soft bed and a restful recuperation were quickly dashed with the descent of newspapermen and shouts of, 'Welcome to America, Mr Dickens.'

Crowds pressed forward to come on board and greet the famous English author. While I was desperate to escape, Charles rose to the occasion, delighting in the acknowledgement of his fame. Countless invitations were pressed into our hands and I wondered how I would find the energy to fulfil them all. In a momentary lapse of concentration, I slipped on the gangplank and twisted my ankle. Charles was overcome with embarrassment and after a hissed chastisement, he joked to all in hearing, 'I think that my wife has taken a little too much brandy to warm her through!'

Thomas kindly came to my aid and bound up my foot, despite my protests that I would be fine. When the crowds subsided, we said goodbye to the Swifts and promised that we would visit them in Philadelphia before returning to England. Charles kissed Consuela's hand and whispered something in her ear to which she responded with a giggle.

'It has been an honour to be in your company, Mrs Swift, and Thomas, I think that I should have gone crazy with both pain and boredom if it had not been for you. I thank you for all you have done.'

We stepped into a waiting coach and made our way to a hotel in Boston in the hope that at last we would have a few days' rest before Charles began his round of engagements.

The lobby of the Tremont House hotel brimmed with women of all ages waiting for a glimpse of my husband. I was alarmed to note that they seemed to have completely forgotten what good breeding signified, and called out without any shame, 'Over here, Mr Dickens! Over here, please!'

I did not know whether to be fearful of his being spirited away, or to feel proud that he was mine. I stood and watched with some amusement as his head popped up every so often above the adoring crowd, calling anxiously, 'Are you still there, Kate?'

He was besieged again, this time with requests for an autograph, but when they began calling for locks of his hair, and pulled at his scarf, he made his excuses and broke away.

Over the days and weeks that followed, Charles hardly refused an invitation: he danced with vigour at the 'Boz Ball', spoke stirringly at the Boston Literary Supper and campaigned unceasingly at every opportunity for the copyright agreement that he sought. But it was not as easy as he had thought. While people admired him as a writer, they were not ready to change the laws of their beloved country to suit an outsider. It seemed that Charles had overestimated people's opinion of him.

One morning, he was reading the newspaper over breakfast and dropped his cup with a clatter into its saucer. 'Vulgar! Uneducated! Me?'

I reached for the newspaper. 'Oh dear, that can't be so. Let me see, my love.'

He snatched it from my grasp.

'How can they call me vulgar and common?' he said, straightening his red cravat and smoothing down his purple waistcoat.

A scuffle outside the window caught his attention and when he drew back the curtain he found a group of journalists trying to peer into our bedroom. At that my husband exploded, calling the men the most dreadful names. I cautioned him that it was not wise to do so if he did not want to receive further bad press, but as usual Charles paid no heed to my opinion.

After weeks of endless engagements, Charles announced that he wished to be free from any more commitments and complained that he could no longer bear being public property.

'If I stay in the hotel, Kate, we are bothered by incessant callers. If I go out then I am set upon by hysterical women. I can't even sneeze in private without receiving a hundred letters asking how is my cold!'

By now I was becoming completely exhausted and the more tired I became, the clumsier I seemed to get. My ankle was still bandaged and, once again, I lost my footing alighting a coach, badly bruising my legs. My head ached, my throat was sore from greeting people, but I dared not confide the slightest illness to Charles lest I disappoint him and be labelled a poor companion.

After Philadelphia and Baltimore, we moved across to the west of the country and the long journey gave me time to sleep and recuperate. However, when we arrived in Illinois we met with the most uncivilized conditions. Charles and I were alarmed at the uncouth manners we encountered and the rapid speed at which saliva was projected across our paths everywhere we went. Charles was greeted by the public with complete indifference and within days I noticed a distinct change in his mood. He had realized that there was no glory in being a writer in a place where people could not read, nor any esteem in being a gentleman where society did not exist. It seemed that he could not thrive without public adulation after all, so once again we packed up our luggage and moved on.

We made our way back through Ohio and moved northwards until at last we crossed the border into Canada. In Ontario, one could almost imagine that we were back in England again. The genteel Canadian hospitality made us feel quite at home and we were once more given the most lavish reception. When asked by the British Ambassador, Lord Mulgrave, Charles felt bound to put on an amateur performance for an invited audience. He urged me to take part, saying that it would be fun and although I was reluctant, I was surprised to find myself rather a good actress. 'But is it any wonder?' I reflected, 'For throughout the whole of this tour I have managed to convince my husband that I really am the keenest of travellers!'

The crowning moment of our visit to Canada was a trip to Niagara Falls. I stood in awe at the great thunder of water softened by silvery spray and rainbows.

'Charles, have you ever seen anything so beautiful in all of your life?' But he did not reply.

'Charles?'

He was perfectly still, transfixed as the spray from the falls gently dampened his face. He peered intently at the huge tumble of water and then suddenly caught his breath.

'Charles? What is it, my love? Are you all right?'

A tear fell from his face. 'It's Mary,' he whispered. 'If you look very carefully, you can see her in the spray. She looks just like an angel.'

At last the time came for us to return to England. We had been away from home for five months and it was painful to think about the hours, days and weeks in which I had not laid eyes upon my children. Too tired to accompany Charles to yet another dinner, I found the time to write and tell them of our imminent return.

June 1842

My dearest darlings

Words cannot express how much I miss you. I only wish that you could have been here to see how the crowds have applauded your Papa and how we have been greeted like royalty wherever we go. We have seen the great city of New York, have travelled to the West where there are red Indians and Papa has even been introduced to President Tyler!

It is all so different from England, though, so much empty space and wilderness. Sometimes I have felt as though I am a million miles away from you. But all of that is about to change: we shall shortly be returning to London. Your Papa has bought gifts for you all and has so many exciting stories to tell you. For now continue to be good and we will be back with you very soon.

God bless you, my dears,
Your loving Mama and Papa

CHAPTER TWENTY-THREE

June 1843
Devonshire Terrace

The population of London was swelling and the city was ill prepared for the numbers that had come pouring in. The streets swarmed with people: labourers seeking work, women selling old clothes, street singers, bow-legged beggars, and orphans sitting on the kerb-side – all of them drawn to the great metropolis. People squeezed into every crack and crevice that was fit to provide shelter, no matter how foul and squalid.

The Dickens' household was growing too, but just like our great city, Charles was not coping either. Although our home was large enough to accommodate a family of six and three servants with ease, Charles was continually pressed by the additional demands of caring for his thriftless parents and honouring the habitual debts run up by his brother, Fred. His journal notes on our visit to America had not been received as well as he had hoped, and he had just lost a lawsuit and found himself responsible for the costs, so when I found out that I was pregnant again, I kept the knowledge from him for as long as I could.

Emily brushed my hair and remarked that Fred had called again. I dismissed her and limped to the bedroom door; since the accident in Scotland and twisting my ankle in America I felt a certain weakness there at times. The weight that I was gaining did not help either. I felt sure that Charles would soon notice my condition.

I heard raised voices coming from the study downstairs and my heart sank as I realized that Charles and Fred were arguing again.

'That girl deserves better than this. How could you have treated her so shabbily? And with her own sister too!'

It seemed that Fred had not changed for the better while we had been overseas. Without Charles here to keep a watchful eye on him he had almost lost his job at the Treasury several times. Worse still, Fred was engaged to be married, but confessed to Charles that his fiancée's sister was expecting his child; Fred had neither money nor courage to resolve the dilemma. I was dismayed by his ungentlemanly behaviour.

'So now you have the monopoly on morals do you, Brother?' Fred countered with sarcasm in his voice. 'If only those who held you in such high esteem, knew how you walked the streets at night and where you went, what would they think of you then? What, indeed, would Kate think?'

I heard the sound of scuffling, and I imagined that Charles had now grasped Fred by the throat.

'How dare you insinuate—? I have never in my life. . . .'

I heard Fred fall to the floor with a cry. Charles continued to rage, 'I found you a job, damn you, a good one at that – so go and work at it and pull yourself out of the filthy hole you have dug yourself into. . . .'

I closed the door and sighed. I did not wish to hear any more. Charles had every right to be angry, I couldn't deny it; if he wasn't keeping his father out of trouble, then it was Fred. But none of this was helping my situation. How could I find the right time to tell Charles my news? I crossed the room to the window and looked out to the garden in search of tranquillity and inspiration. I noticed how the flowers danced gently in the breeze. I felt that I, too, was being softly lulled by their movement. My head felt hot and strangely light. One by one the flowers formed a circle and danced a ring o' roses around me.

My ears rang with the echo of angry voices. The flowers turned their faces to me and each one became the face of a new born-baby calling, 'Mama, Mama', over and over. Their leaves became chubby little arms that stretched out and embraced me, squeezing the breath out of me until gradually I was enveloped by darkness.

I awoke, and the familiar shapes and shadows of my bedroom came into focus. I reached out my hands in an attempt to orientate myself and felt the silky covers of the eiderdown beneath my fingertips. Over by the window Charles and Dr Bell were conversing in a low tone.

'Charles?' I called softly.

He turned and immediately I saw a weariness of expression that could not hide his despair at the prospect of another child.

'Remember,' Dr Bell cautioned, 'she must rest.'

The doctor left and Charles knelt down at the side of the bed and took my hand. He attempted to smile, but his eyes betrayed his sadness. Then he took a breath as if he were about to say something reassuring, but for once the man of great words struggled to create a fiction for my benefit. His eyes met mine and the sadness in them turned to fear.

'Kate,' he whispered, gripping the bed covers, 'I am afraid that we shall be ruined.'

Some months later, Charles decided that we would rent out our home and live in Italy for a while. He reasoned that it would be cheaper to live abroad and I would agree to anything that I thought might raise his spirits and give me some respite from his moodiness. To his friends, however, he kept up a show of bravado and boasted, 'Of course, in Italy I shall write as I have never written before. I shall be inspired by its grandeur and beauty. I might even rent a castle!'

Upon our arrival in Genoa, we did indeed take up rooms in a small castle in the countryside, but beyond the heavy oak door the grandeur and beauty ceased. Inside, the building was crumbling, draughty and dark and it was not at all suitable for the children. Charles, however, had other concerns: deprived of warmth and light he could not find inspiration at all, and he quickly uprooted us and moved us to a villa in the city. Here at last we found light, warmth and enough room for a large family and its domestics. I felt relieved that we were settled.

Charles, however, was not at all settled. He paced about, still dissatisfied; his writing implements had not arrived from England and no other desk would suffice. He was always very particular about such matters. First he would position his desk overlooking a view, then he would take great care to lay out every item upon it in a certain way until he was satisfied. Once arranged, he would insist that he and he alone was the only one to sit at it, and that nothing on it should be touched. It seemed he believed that if anything should be altered or disturbed in any way that his whole world would disappear and the spell of his success would be broken. When the crate eventually arrived and he had personally unpacked all his things and laid out them just so, he sat in his study for the rest of the day.

'At last he is at peace,' I sighed with relief. 'Now I shall be at peace too.'

But when he was called for his supper, he came out of his study ashen and trembling.

'Charles, whatever is the matter?' I asked with great consternation.

He threw his hands up in despair. 'It has happened, Kate. Just as I always feared.'

'What has happened, my love?' I asked gently, not wanting to provoke his anger.

'I couldn't write a thing, Kate. Not one word.'

'Perhaps you are tired, dearest.'

'No, it is not that at all!' he snapped, pacing backwards and forwards across the hallway. 'I need the streets of London for my inspiration. Unless we return, I am finished.'

He grasped his hair in exasperation, snatched up his walking cane and went out of the front door. I watched him walk down the narrow sloped street, talking to himself and gesturing wildly.

I began to panic, *Oh, dear God, no – please don't let him move us again. I could not bear it.*

When evening came, and the children were all asleep, he returned. He danced up the path, whistling a tune from an Italian opera and conducted an imaginary orchestra with his cane. I came across the hall about to remonstrate with him for drinking too much and he beamed at the sight of me.

'Kate, I've got it!' He swung me around and kissed my forehead.

'Charles, let me go,' I laughed, relieved at his good temper.

'Not until you listen to my idea. It can't go wrong.'

I began to open my mouth in protest at his grip on me.

'Shhhh!' he whispered, putting his hand gently to my lips, 'Listen.'

'Listen to what?' I implored.

'Listen,' he repeated, pointing outside.

The peal of the church bells rang out, becoming louder and clearer upon my recognition of them.

'*The Chimes*!' he laughed. 'That's my story – just like the bells of St Martin in the Fields back home. I've found my inspiration, Kate. I've found it!' He swung me around again and again, laughing joyously.

CHAPTER TWENTY-FOUR

July 1844
Genoa, Italy

'I feel more alive here, Kate, than anywhere else in the world.'

Charles walked out onto the bedroom balcony and stretched out his arms above his head, inhaling the sea air deep into his lungs. 'In coming away from the familiar, I feel that every sense that I possess has taken on renewed vitality.' He leaned upon the iron railings and looked out at the old town below. 'My imagination is teased by what I might find when I walk along those twisting alleyways, Kate, and my eyes are delighted by all these colourful houses bathed in sunlight.'

I followed him out onto the balcony and rested my hand lightly on his shoulder. I was pleased to see him relaxed for once. 'Are you not working today, my love?'

'No, I thought that I might walk over to see Augusta and see how she is this morning.'

My hand fell away from his shoulder.

'Again?' I said with dismay.

Augusta de la Rue was the beautiful wife of a local banker in the city. She had frequently invited Charles and me to her home to dine with many of her other influential circle. Her husband, Emile, was a quiet man and it was apparent that he was utterly devoted to his vivacious wife and would do anything to find a cure for her 'troubles'. One evening he confided to Charles, 'You would think to look at her now, that she is as sane as you or I, but, when we are alone she imagines that we are being watched everywhere we go. By day she falls into the most terrible fits and by night she endures the most terrifying nightmares. I have consulted the best physicians in Europe, but as yet no one can find the cause of her anxiety.'

After dinner, Charles performed some of his favourite conjuring tricks and Madam de la Rue clapped her hands with enthusiasm: 'You know, Mr Dickens, I am convinced that you really are able to work magic and I think that were you to lay your hands upon *me*, you could make me well again.' She fluttered her fingers as if casting a spell and laughed.

With an inflated opinion of his own power Charles took her at her word and promised to call upon her again and do what he could to help her.

On the way home, I berated him. 'In heaven's name, why did you go and put such an idea in her head.'

He threw me a look of indignation. 'I think that I could do it, Kate, I really do.'

By now he had completed *The Chimes* and was determined to return to England to read it to his friends – their approbation was a necessary as ever to his ego – but he remained firm in his resolve to call upon Madam de la Rue upon his return. He left me with strict instructions to touch nothing in his study and to leave everything just as it was. A week later he wrote and told of the success of his reading:

There was not a dry eye in the place, Kate. I feel that it is a marvellous thing to have such power and it has caused me to think again about the request made by Madam de la Rue. I believe more than ever that perhaps she is right and I truly do possess the power to make her well, and I confess that I cannot think of anything else. . . .

Any*one* else! I thought bitterly, crushing his letter in my hand.

It was obvious to me now that he was driven by one thought and one thought alone. There was only one subject in the world to him now, and that subject was Augusta de la Rue and it bewitched and possessed him. Impelled by the obsession, he returned to Italy with great haste and called upon her the moment he set foot back in Genoa.

When he came home – without even a word of greeting – he enthused, 'Kate, you will never believe it! I called upon Madam de la Rue just as I said I would, and all I did was to lay my hands gently upon her and she fell asleep. I spent the whole afternoon by her side and, when she awoke, she proclaimed it to be the most peaceful sleep that she had experienced in months, and that I must attend her again tomorrow.'

I bristled with resentment, 'And what of your family? We have not seen you in weeks. Will you not attend to us?'

But he was not listening. He headed for his study, shaking his head and looking at his hands, turning them backwards and forwards. 'Amazing!' he muttered. 'Simply amazing!'

Each day thereafter, Charles called upon Madam de la Rue and spent long days in her company. He wrote detailed notes of their discussions together and about the success of his 'treatment'.

When the de la Rues next travelled to Rome, Emile insisted that we must accompany them too, lest Augusta feel unwell and need to call upon Charles at any time.

'She is like a different woman when you are around, my friend.'

I was amazed at Emile's acceptance of this strange charade.

One night, Charles awoke at two in the morning and leapt from the bed calling her name, 'Augusta!' He hopped around in the darkness, trying to put his foot into his trouser leg.

'What on earth are you doing?' I asked, imagining that he was dreaming.

'I must go to her, she needs me – I can just feel it.'

He grabbed his coat and scarf from the wardrobe.

'What do you mean she needs you? How can she need you at

this time of night?'

'I sense it. She is calling out for me – I have to go to her. I will return as soon as I can, Kate. Go back to sleep.' He slipped on his shoes and in a moment he had gone.

I rose from the bed and went out onto the balcony, watching the nimble figure of my husband disappearing into the night. Sleep? How could I sleep when the man I loved appeared to be at the complete beck and call of another woman, whose every need he was putting ahead of my own? Why did Emile not say something? Why could he not see what was going on? But what *was* going on? Charles appeared convinced that he had some kind of efficacy over Madam de la Rue's disturbed mind, but was it merely the sense of power it gave him which drove him to her side, or was there more?

The following morning over breakfast, Charles did not seem to notice my silence and talked of nothing but Augusta. I felt my fingers tighten around the handle of my tea cup.

He took a bite of his pastry, 'Do you know, Kate, when I got to the de la Rue residence I found the poor woman curled up in a tight ball at the foot of her bed, moaning and sobbing uncontrollably.'

He took a sip of his coffee.

'Yes, dear Emile was beside himself with despair, but when he saw me, Kate, he took me by the hand, shaking it with a gratitude pitiful to see. "*My dear Charles, thank God that you are here. She has been like this for most of the night and I dared not leave her side to send word to you. What in the world is wrong with her?*"

'So I told him, Kate' – there was another bite of his pastry – 'allow me some time alone with her and I will do what I can.'

My fingers increased their pressure on the handle of the tea cup.

'Well, I spent most of the night with her, and when I later emerged from the room, closing the door quietly behind me, I was able to comfort Emile, "*She is sleeping now, dear fellow, but I will stay by her bedside if you will permit it, so that I will be close at hand in case of any further distress*".' He popped the final piece of pastry into his

139

mouth and took his napkin from his lap to wipe his lips.

'When I left this morning, I told him that I would return again after lunch, to see how she is faring. I reassured Emile, "*No trouble, no trouble at all. . . .*" '

With a final squeeze of my finger and thumb the handle snapped and the cup clattered into the saucer, splashing tea all over my dressing-gown.

'Kate, you really are clumsy! Whatever were you thinking of?'

When the holiday in Rome was over and we returned to Genoa, I hoped that my husband's thoughts would turn in another direction, but still he called upon that woman without missing a day, and I began to determine that I must say something or go mad with rage. One evening, I watched him through the crack in our bedroom door. He stood in front of the mirror and was holding a piece of hair between the finger and thumb of one hand and a pair of scissors in the other, his tongue protruding from the side of his mouth in concentration.

I walked into the room unannounced. 'What in heaven's name are you doing?'

He jumped at my unexpected entrance, the scissors spinning from his hand.

'Good God, Kate! You startled me. I could have done myself an injury.'

He bent down to retrieve them. I noticed an open locket on the dressing table and a surge of jealousy pulsed through my veins.

'*Who* is that for?'

'It is nothing!' he retorted, and snatched up the trinket, snapping it shut. 'An admirer asked for a lock of my hair. A silly token; it's nothing more than that.'

I looked at his well-kept curls and said with derision, 'Am I to believe that you would disturb a hair on your head in the cause of a meaningless token?'

'Believe what you will, Kate, but if you insist on knowing its purpose it is intended for Augusta. It is purely for medicinal purposes; when she is not in my company she finds herself failing again and her old trouble returns. I thought that if she had something of me about her person it might help her in my absence.'

He tucked the locket away in his pocket hoping that its disappearance might end our disagreement.

'And what are you going to do when the locket is no longer sufficient? Are you going to snip away at your clothing piece by piece and give her that too?' I was aware that I was raising my voice in tearful agitation.

'Now you are being ridiculous.' He looked at his reflection and patted down his curls.

'Women like that are never satisfied until they possess you body and soul,' my voice wavered.

He turned abruptly and looked upon me with disdain. 'You have no right to talk of Augusta in that way. Good God, Kate! Show some compassion; the woman is ill and I have the capacity to make her well. Can you conceive how that feels? The power to make someone well again? Whereas you, you have the capacity for being unreasonably suspicious and selfish.'

'Selfish! How can you say such a thing when I have sat by and watched you lavish every minute of your spare time upon this woman and yet said nothing. Even when you left me in the middle of the night to go to her, I said nothing. But now I am saying that this obsession must stop. I will no longer be humiliated in this way.'

'And tell me, who will be humiliated when I have to tell Madam de la Rue that I can no longer call upon her because my *wife* has demanded it? What will her husband think then? He will think that I have something to hide. He will think that I am not master in my own house.'

'And do you have something to hide?'

He clenched and unclenched his fist. 'You are testing me, Kate. Testing me beyond what you should. You do not know your place when you ask me such a thing.'

'What he thinks should not matter to you. What should matter is the feelings of your wife!'

141

A dark look entered his eyes and for a moment I thought that he might seize me by the throat. It was a look of bitter resentment, but, without a word, he turned and left the room.

What was said to the de la Rues I do not know, but after that day Charles no longer sought their company nor they ours. At last I was relieved of the burden of his unrelenting obsession, but I was soon to realize that this was not to be his last.

CHAPTER TWENTY-FIVE

June 1845
London, England

'London has not changed one bit,' Charles complained bitterly within days of returning to England. 'I miss the sunshine, the beauty of the Italian countryside and already I'm bored!'

He sniffed miserably into his handkerchief. He had come down with a heavy cold and not even the decoration that he had ordered for the house while we had been away could cheer his mood. As for me, I had begun to notice that I did not feel myself at all and that I carried with me a great sense of unease wherever I went. However, I did not attempt to voice my worries to Charles; I was with child again and he looked upon me scornfully as if it were entirely my fault, so there was little use in asking for his sympathy.

He wandered over to the drawing-room window and looked out wearily at a view he had seen a hundred times before. 'This house has no life in it – it needs brightening: noise, visitors, anything to take away this dreary monotony.'

'I say, you there, old fellow, what is your business here?' Charles called suddenly.

A vagabond carrying a bundle had hurried past the house, fearful that, having slipped by the porter at the gates, his presence would soon be discovered. The man looked up with supplication in his eyes, and opened his coat, revealing the bundle to be a child. Hearing that Charles Dickens lived in this street, the man had hoped that he might discover the whereabouts of the great author and that he might be pitied, and a coin dropped in his hand. The spirit of charity, so often in the centre of my husband's heart, whispered to his conscience that he should do something; and Charles threw the man a coin and a wish for God's blessing upon him and his child. My husband closed the window and I watched as his face grew pale and he visibly shuddered; it was not with repulsion, but with fear, as if he had seen a vision of how life might have turned out for him, and how life might still turn out if he let his hand rest for even a moment.

He began to wring his hands and said, with agitation in his voice, 'I must work, Kate, I need a project, a new idea – I have to work. I must!'

And so he shut himself away and began writing, sketching out ideas, creating an imaginary world that only he controlled.

Unbeknown to me he had also begun making domestic plans.

The doorbell rang and Charles's face brightened. He looked at his watch.

'Ten o'clock precisely,' he beamed. 'Capital!'

I wondered who Charles could be expecting so early in the morning. Perhaps it was the artist, Daniel Maclise. He had recently lost his mother and had become a changed man; no longer dashing about London pursuing unsuitable women. He had become depressed, withdrawn, refusing to paint or draw. Charles had taken a brotherly interest in him and had told him to call anytime night or day. Charles also planned to produce a series of benefit performances with a view to raising funds for artists who had fallen on hard times, and thought that Mr Maclise might be aided by such a fund.

I looked in the mirror, wondering if I was presentable enough to receive an unexpected guest, but with disappointment I found a stranger looking back at me: dark shadows lay in the deepening creases beneath my eyes and I pinched my cheeks trying to bring some colour to my pale complexion. A tendril of grey hung down from my temple and I hurriedly attempted to blend it in with the darker strands, tucking it behind my ear.

Leaving the bedroom, I paused for a moment at the top of the staircase. I could hear Charles talking with great excitement and the voice of a woman laughing in response.

'Charles, you are too kind. What beautiful flowers!'

'And you, young miss, are every bit as fresh and as lovely as they are. In fact, I do declare that you are lovelier than when I last set eyes upon you!'

I stepped quietly down the stairs and found Charles in the hallway, his eyes shining, holding onto both hands of my young sister, Georgie, who was by now quite the young woman. He looked up at me saying, 'Kate, I have a surprise for you. I told you that the house needed cheering up, so I have invited Georgie to come to stay with us.'

I smiled. 'Well, we will be very pleased to have you, dear, and the children will enjoy having you with us for a few weeks, won't they, Charles?'

Charles blinked for a second. 'Kate, you have completely misunderstood: your sister will be staying with us for good.'

With a flood of disquiet, memories came rushing back at me as if the years had fallen away, and all my old fears surrounded me once more. I took hold of the string of pearls that hung around my neck and began to twist them around my fingers with great agitation.

'No, no . . . it cannot be. . . . What do you mean, for good? I'm really not sure—'

'Not sure? What is wrong with you, Kate? You are not making sense at all. It is very simple: now that Georgie has completed her schooling, she will be a great aid to the children in their own studies, can't you see? And with you, er . . . well, in your customary condition, you will be glad of the help, *won't you?*' His final two words were more like a direct instruction.

Georgie, who had become preoccupied with rearranging some flowers that I had set in a vase upon the hall table, seemed completely untroubled by my cool reception, as if she had not an ounce of sensitivity in her bones at all.

'Now, where were we, ah, yes. . . .' Charles nodded at Georgie's floral artistry with approval and then linked arms with her and strolled across the hall. 'Wait 'til you see my growing library. Your knowledge of the world is only just beginning, young lady, but I myself shall teach you everything else you will ever need to know.' Charles sighed with contentment and patted her hand, 'Do you realize, Georgie, all my dreams that have lain unfulfilled will now be fulfilled by you? Now come, tell me, which room would you like? And when you have unpacked we will go for a long walk.'

Remembering my presence in the hall, Charles turned back for a moment and said in wonder, 'Do you know, Kate, I don't think that there is a man who can match me stride for stride like your sister can.'

He turned back again to Georgie. 'Ah, yes, now that you are here, everything will be in order again, Mary. . . .'

He faltered, realizing his mistake.

'Yes,' I whispered inaudibly. 'Back from the dead!'

CHAPTER TWENTY-SIX

June 1846
Devonshire Terrace, London

Our sixth child was another son – Alfred d'Orsay Tennyson Dickens. Tennyson so named for my husband's favourite poet, and d'Orsay after the charming French count.

A summer ball was to be held at the count's place of residence, Gore House, and although I felt less than fit to attend, I did so as a means of staying close to my husband's side. After all, who would he meet there? I would have no way of knowing. The experience with Madam de la Rue in Genoa had been unnerving, and left me with a lasting feeling of vulnerability.

Charles stood before the cheval glass and, in turn, held in front of him a red waistcoat and then a purple.

'Which do you think, Kate? The red brocade or the purple silk?'

'The red, my dear?' I ventured.

He held the brocade waistcoat against him and his features condensed into a frown. Shaking his head, he tossed the garment onto the bed and began putting on the purple one with a nod of satisfaction. I was in my customary condition, once again, and was very conscious that my gown strained noticeably around my ever-expanding waistline. There was nothing for it, I would have to keep my mantle on all evening.

When we arrived at Gore House, I felt my anxiety heighten,

observing through the carriage window the large crowd of guests streaming through the Palladian pillars and into the grand hall. I began to twist at my pearls, but Count d'Orsay was as charming as ever and managed to put me at my ease immediately.

'You are looking very radiant this evening, madam, if your husband will allow me to say so.'

'You are always so kind, Alfred, thank you.'

'And how are. . . ?'

His unaffected small talk came to an abrupt end at the entrance of the hostess into the ballroom: a woman of beautiful form, so ethereal that she appeared to be a fancy of one's imagination. His face took on a look of complete contentment and a smile played about his lips.

'You love her very much, don't you?' I whispered.

He opened up his heart without a moment's hesitation. 'With my very being.'

Lady Blessington, had been born Miss Margaret Power, in County Wicklow, Ireland. The child of a harsh man who, without a thought for his poor daughter's feelings, had handed her over in marriage at the age of fifteen to a captain in the army. The young girl's circumstances were not at all improved for she found that her worthless husband drank heavily and had run up many debts. Her relief can only be imagined when his dissolute life came to an end during a drunken brawl, and she fled to England, where she met the recently widowed Earl of Blessington. Captivated by Margaret's natural beauty, and deciding that his daughter was in need of a maternal figure, he quickly married her and bestowed upon his new wife the title Marguerite, Lady Blessington.

Lord Blessington not only had an eye for beauty but also a taste for luxury and enjoyed purchasing exotic items. Marguerite adapted to her new life with great ease and enthusiasm and accompanied her husband and stepdaughter all over Europe. It was in France where they were all to meet Count d'Orsay, and no woman could deny that the young count was handsome, kind and intelligent; but more than that he had the ability to make the oldest dowager feel like a young girl again. Lady Blessington fell hopelessly in love. But what complicated relations were to ensue: Lord Blessington settled a dowry of £40,000 upon his daughter, if the dashing Frenchman were to marry her. The count, who in turn had fallen in love with Marguerite, could not bear to be parted from her, and felt compelled to agree, as a means of staying at her side.

Just two years later the elderly Lord Blessington died, his daughter abandoned the count, and went to Europe, and d'Orsay was subsequently left in the family home with his widowed stepmother.

'Have you plans to travel this summer, d'Orsay?' My husband had now joined us in the ballroom.

'Marguerite wishes us to travel to Italy, and of course, whatever Marguerite wishes. . . .' the count smiled fondly. 'And you, sir?'

Charles looked at me somewhat resentfully. 'Well, I had wanted to return to Genoa myself, but Kate has requested that we go to Switzerland, instead.'

He lowered his voice as if I could not hear him. 'My wife is a little unsettled in her mind at present, so I have to indulge her wishes, d'Orsay, you know how it is with women.'

July 1846
Lausanne, Switzerland

Charles looked at his pocket watch and beamed. His eyes sparkled with approval as Georgie stood in the hall next to a row of spotless children and a neat stack of luggage.

'Eight a.m. on the dot. Capital, Georgie! Capital!'

He threw a look of despair my way, casting a glance at a large bump above my eye. In my haste to be ready, I had tripped on the bedroom rug and caught my head on the corner of the dressing table. Charles raised his eyebrows and enquired in a sarcastic tone, 'Kate, do you think that you might actually manage to board the coach without bruising, twisting or spraining anything?'

The children suppressed a chorus of muffled giggles, and Georgie hurried them along out of the door.

Charley was not among our travelling party as he was now at boarding school, hard at his education. Miss Burdett-Coutts had persuaded Charles to allow her to pay for Charley's schooling, she being aware of the unpredictable nature of my husband's earnings.

'Think of it as a loan, if you wish, my dear Dickens, but I would prefer to think of it as a thank you for the giving of yourself unceasingly to my charity work.'

Charles reluctantly acquiesced, swallowing his pride in order to give to his son the education that he himself had been denied. The knowledge of this had helped me to understand the great drive for work that propelled my husband through life. However, that great drive now dragged along with it myself and the children. Although I resented Georgie's intrusion into my life, I was glad that she was to accompany us on our travels, I was tired of it all.

I found Lausanne to be a clean little city, the hillsides dotted with pretty wooden cottages and the mountains intersected by streams. As a family we settled very well there. Not long after we had arrived, however, we received a letter from home bearing bad news. Fanny was failing in health. She had developed consumption and was not rallying at all.

'I must return at once to see her,' Charles said in distress, pushing the letter into his waistcoat pocket.

I hesitated, uncertain if I was expected to accompany him, but thankfully Charles did not mention it, and within the morning he had packed and was gone.

The following month, when Charles returned, he wore an

expression of controlled fear.

'Is it really so very bad, my dear?' I enquired sensitively.

My husband took me gently but purposefully by the arm and led me to a chair.

'Charles. . . ?'

He cleared his throat several times, 'Kate, you must be very brave. I have something very serious to tell you.'

A mixture of fear and confusion swept over me. He knew how I felt about Fanny, so what could be so awful? I sat down, glad of the chair beneath me.

'Kate, it's Charley . . . no, don't give way; remember, I said that you must be very brave.' He gripped my hands tightly. 'He has scarlet fever and the doctor says . . . you must be brave, Kate, the doctor says that . . . that . . . he may not recover.'

I got up and began wringing my hands in despair. 'Oh, dear lord, we must go to him, Charles, before it is too late.'

'It is impossible, Kate; you will never survive the journey in such a state of distress. If you cannot think of yourself, think of the child that you are carrying. It is too great a risk to both of you.'

How could he remain so impassive? 'But this is our son, Charles, our own flesh and blood. This is not a character from one of your books, you cannot control his fate with a stroke of your pen. This is real and we must face the truth with feelings. You cannot escape from what is happening any more that I can.' I had made him angry now.

'That is enough, Kate! I have made my decision. We will stay here and trust that Dr Bell will employ every means necessary to aid Charley's recovery.'

After this he forbade me to speak further on the subject and would not bend at all, only saying that everything would be well if we stayed strong. But my spirit was broken and I withdrew into a dark, shadowy world where sun did not break through and pain lay upon my heart like a biting frost. As Charles remained firm in his refusal to talk about Charley, the days and weeks that followed were unbearably lonely with only terror as

151

my constant companion. I was unreasonably fearful for the safety of my other children and unable to sleep or eat. Every letter that came was both a feared enemy and a welcome friend.

I sat now in the drawing room and was disturbed in my reverie by young Katie who looked at me with some perplexity upon her rounded face.

'Mama, are you quite all right?' I had not heard her enter the room at all, and so she repeated her question. 'Mama?'

Suddenly I became aware of her presence and looked down to find that I had wound my string of pearls so tightly around my forefingers, that, lost in my thoughts, my fingers had begun to redden with constriction. I relaxed my grip and made a conscious effort to focus my attention on the anxious child looking up at me.

'Have you been standing there long, my dear?' I asked suddenly feeling very cold.

'No, Mama, only a moment.'

I looked over my shoulder and then back at Katie.

'I had the strangest sensation that someone was watching me and that they stroked my cheek.'

Her little face formed a worried frown. 'Do you want me to call Papa or Aunt Georgie, for you, Mama?'

'No, no, dear; I am quite all right. Run along and play, and do not worry yourself about Mama. I am fine.' I ruffled her hair and she skipped away, concerned no more.

At last the news that I had prayed for arrived and I can only give thanks to God that my eldest son survived his illness. Fanny, however, in a reversal of fortune was not so blessed. Charles wrote daily for news of her condition and when it seemed that all hope had gone, he insisted that we return to England so that "his presence in person might give her strength beyond what was normal". Perhaps in saying this he had in mind his experiences with Madam de la Rue, as if he had the power even over life and death.

We arrived home at Devonshire Terrace at the end of November and while I prepared for Charley's return home for

Christmas, Charles rushed immediately to Fanny's side. For some months his presence seemed to have some miraculous effect on her after all, and temporarily she gained strength and comfort from her brother's presence. But not even my husband's great fame could frighten death's dark shadow from Fanny's side and Charles was prostrated by grief at the loss of his sister.

As one life left the world, so another entered it. Our son Sydney was born and I was now the mother of seven children.

CHAPTER TWENTY-SEVEN

Autumn 1849
Brompton Asylum, London

William tapped the roof of the carriage and asked the driver to stop.

'This will do, there's no need for him to know where we are going,' he whispered, twisting his wedding-ring nervously. We stepped down and William reminded him to be sure to meet us in the same place in an hour.

'Right you are, guv'nor.' He touched his cap and shook the reins.

William Thackeray was a man of large stature, with cherubic curls and a kind and handsome face, upon which sat a slightly lopsided nose. In all the time that I had known William I had never known him raise his voice, lose his temper or speak ill of others. Some thought him false, perhaps too good to be true, but I saw him as he was – a man of good breeding who would think it ill-mannered to show anything other than a congenial nature at all times, whatever his true feelings.

In contrast to Charles, he had experienced the privileged upbringing of a gentleman. Born in India to a wealthy father, William had enjoyed the comforts of a magnificent home: servants to wash him, dress him and wait upon him, and an exotic countryside as his own playground. But his charmed life was to come to an abrupt end. His father died suddenly and William's mother quickly married her lover, sending William to a boarding-school. It was here, I think, that he had had his nose broken by a boy for whom he ran errands.

The unhappy years of his youth had been marked by a lack of purpose: he gambled recklessly, and could not settle upon a career that made him happy.

His mother – too wrapped up in her own world – denied him much needed affection and, it was whispered, that his frequent visits to houses of ill-repute had left him with a lasting legacy that still came back to trouble him at times.

But when William met Isabella, he found the happiness that had evaded him since the death of his father and his life of aimlessness ended. His income as a fledgling journalist paid for a small cottage and lack of money did not taint the sweetness of their love for one another; he and Isabella settled down to become the happiest couple I knew. His career as a journalist was now flourishing, his skill as an illustrator was growing – he would often amuse us with his delightful caricatures drawn upon napkins – and his name as an author was becoming respected.

So it was all the more cruel that life had looked upon him unkindly once more. Jane, the middle of their three young daughters, had died in infancy from pneumonia, and after the recent birth of another daughter, Harriet, Isabella had become lower and lower in her spirits. Perhaps she feared that she would lose dear Harriet too. William had taken his wife overseas in the hope that a change of scenery would do her health some good, but the consequences were tragic: during the crossing, Isabella had thrown herself from the boat and almost drowned.

It was some few weeks later that I found myself seated opposite him in a carriage, with Emily, the maid, at my side. For the most part of the journey he was distracted, looking out of the window, lost in thought. From time to time he would remember his manners and turn to address me, enquiring about my comfort or making a general comment about the weather. In his vacant moments he directed his forefinger to trace a repeated hieroglyph on his thigh. I followed, watching the long stroke of an 'I', followed by S . . . A . . . then the remainder of his wife's name. Over and over he traced it. Poor William, he blamed himself I knew, and yet no one could have known. Isabella had hidden her sadness so well, too well in fact, until she could hold it in no longer.

Leaving Emily in the coach to wait for our return, we walked along a labyrinth of narrow streets: children played hopscotch, housekeepers hurried along with their baskets, workmen loaded beer barrels onto a cart, a policeman kept pace with an imaginary beat. Side by side I walked with William, talking of everything except that which we could not put into words – the fear of what we were about to do. We came at last to a partly derelict building surrounded by a high wall that was topped with spikes. Forged in iron above the gate were the words Brompton Asylum. It was manned by a guard who must have been nearer seven feet than six. He had large ears, and due to a lack of teeth his jaw sat comfortably under his nose. He looked like an enormous grey gnome guarding his mine. He eyed us suspiciously. It was rumoured that a well-dressed lunatic had once walked out of the asylum leaving his poor brother, who had come to visit, tied up in his place. Our identities satisfactorily established, he let us in and led us to the twin-towered gatehouse and entrance. Between the towers was a large oak door and chiselled above it in the stone: *Nil Desperandum – Auspice Deum*. William shook his cane angrily. 'Bah! God is not in this place, I'm sure of it. Suffering – yes, pain – yes, but not God.'

I started to say that God is everywhere if only we believed and looked hard enough, but upon entering the dark vestibule my words trailed off. Moans of torment, shrieks, insane chatter and a repetitive banging; the echoes of torment resonated throughout the building. The smell of dampness permeated the air. The draughty hall was empty of people and furniture, the only adornments being a memorial stone giving thanks to the patrons of the asylum, and on the opposite wall – a metal crucifix. We heard the sound of footsteps; a man, small and rounded, approached us. He was dressed in a rather shabby shirt, tie and waistcoat, and his sleeves were rolled up as though he had hastily left a job unfinished to greet us.

'Mr Thackeray?' he said, in a weary tone.

William nodded.

'I am Doctor Hargreaves.'

His face was careworn and there seemed to be a line upon his brow for every patient he had ever tended.

'My wife, where is she?' William asked, taking off his hat and gloves.

'Mr Thackeray,' the doctor said, without answering William's question, 'would you mind if I asked you to step into the office?'

'Doctor, I have not come here to talk, nor have I come to sit in your office. I have come to see my wife and I want to see her now!' He lowered his voice and added, 'If you please', remembering his customary manners.

The doctor had witnessed this scene many times before and would see it again. He could be patient; within these walls time moved very slowly.

'This won't take a moment, sir.' He gestured toward an open door leading off the hall. 'If you would?' And William, temporarily defeated, stepped into the room.

The doctor nodded to the chairs positioned in front of a desk, and while I took mine, William declined with a frown and a shake of his head. A small bookcase held a collection of medical books, whose only purpose seemed to be to gather dust. Heavy wooden panelling added to the room's air of darkness, the light coming in two sharp shafts from the tall windows that were barred like all the others I had seen. Doctor Hargreaves carefully rolled down his sleeves, sat himself behind the desk and began looking through each drawer, taking out a file, shaking his head and returning it to its place. A piece of thread dangled from his worn cuffs and it waved and danced as he slowly shuffled and

157

arranged his papers causing me to want to snap it off with irritation. At last he found what he was looking for, looked over the notes and peering above his spectacles, said grimly, 'I am afraid to tell you, Mr Thackeray, that your wife has ceased to function as the woman you once knew. The loss of the child has troubled her deeply, and she has become withdrawn, shutting out reality all together.'

William wrung his hands and paced the room as though he himself were on the edge of insanity. He shook a finger at the doctor. 'My wife was put here without my authority, you know that, don't you? I came home to find that this terrible outrage had taken place and if I had thought for one moment that this was going to happen, I should never have left her unattended. She is my life, sir.'

The doctor nodded sympathetically, 'But I'm sure you appreciate that the police had little choice, Mr Thackeray. Your wife tried to take a child from another woman and, when questioned she held fast to the belief that the infant was her own.' He took off his glasses and said plainly, 'I'm afraid, sir, that your wife might not recover her senses at all. I hope that with the very best treatment, we may be able to reach her, but I cannot promise.'

William, putting his hands on the desk, leaned forward earnestly and said, 'Then you must let me try, and Mrs Dickens here, whom she regards so fondly.'

'She will not even know you, Mr Thackeray, I am sure of it,' the doctor insisted. 'Seeing her will only cause you both unnecessary distress.'

'I will not be dissuaded,' William continued, 'and I will not agree to my wife being experimented upon by some kind of . . . quack, and dosed with heaven knows what sort of ill potions!'

William mopped his face and neck with his handkerchief, not at all used to losing his composure, but this was not at all a usual circumstance. Doctor Hargreaves stood up and, ignoring William's outburst, nodded saying, 'Very well then, it seems you must see for yourself.'

Leaving the office we walked along a dimly lit corridor, passing strange beings who practised strange rituals. I am not sure whether it was a man or a woman, but a bald headed creature sat crossed-legged, trying to remove an imaginary speck from it's tongue. With finger and thumb it plucked repeatedly, never giving up for a moment, to the point where I too believed that it must be there and thought that it would be a kindness on my part to help remove it. The long corridor was white tiled, windowless, and flagged along the way with heavy doors. I was terrified by the thought of what horrors lay behind them and yet, was not my dear Isabella one of these poor sick creatures? I reminded myself that I must not judge.

At the end of the tunnel was a door with a small barred window in it. As we drew near to it the doctor raised a hand, momentarily halting us. 'Sir, if you are really sure you want to go through with this. . . .'

'Whatever has happened to her, she will never be changed in my eyes,' William countered with emotion.

The doctor did not unlock the door immediately, but directed us to look through its small barred window. William stepped forward and put his face to the bars and after a moment of shock, closed his eyes with pain.

'It's all right,' I whispered, clasping his arm and glancing over his shoulder through to the small cell beyond the window. 'We have come this far, William, now let us see what can be done.'

Crouched against the cell wall was Isabella. She was wearing the wine-coloured dress that I had seen her in many times before but now it was heavily stained. Her hair hung loosely about her shoulders and had turned completely white and on her left hand was a fresh wound that looked like a bite mark. She appeared to be cradling a bundle of rags in her arms and when I looked closer I could see that it was a doll to which she was quietly talking. Her voice was soft and familiar and although she looked unrecognizable she sounded like Isabella in every respect. The doctor unlocked the door and, with hope rising, I moved toward her. Immediately she bit viciously at her hand and huddled into

159

a corner of the cell, clutching her bundle and becoming breathless with fear.

'Don't try to take her from me, you bitch, I warn you!'

Her voice had become distorted and strange. I looked down at the doll and felt sickened to see that its eyes were merely empty sockets in a filthy face. Trying to keep my mind clear, I petitioned, 'Izzy, William is here. Look, he has come to take you home.'

He crouched down carefully and said tentatively, 'My dear?'

She looked at him blankly and then began to shriek and grasp at my skirts. 'The baby, he's going to take it, miss; dear God – don't let him please. Please!' She clawed again. 'Make him go!' She released my skirt and began ripping great clumps of hair from her scalp, seemingly oblivious to the pain.

'Sir, you must come away, she is becoming overwrought!' the doctor urged William. The noise that she was making was unbearable to hear, like an animal trapped in the jaws of a beast.

'No! You must do something. Somebody must do something. I can't leave her like this,' William pleaded.

Isabella launched herself at her husband and began tearing at his face, sinking her nails into his flesh. With an experienced hand, the doctor swiftly took a shackle from the cell wall clasped it around Isabella's neck and herded us out, locking the door with great haste.Almost immediately Isabella fell to the floor and became quiet again, singing softly to her baby as though we had never encroached upon her world at all. William's complexion was white and he dabbed at his marked face. Seeing the blood on his fingertips, he turned away with a violent cough and I thought that he was about to vomit. Doctor Hargreaves put a hand on his shoulder.

'I'm sorry for you, sir, truly I am, but if you will pay her board of fifteen shillings a week, I will ensure that your wife is moved to a better part of the hospital and will employ a nurse for her who will see to it that she is washed and well fed – and of course, I will make every treatment available to hasten her cure. That is all far more than most of the poor souls here could ever hope for.'

William nodded vaguely, but I do not think that it was in acknowledgement of the doctor's words for he seemed too numb with shock to comprehend speech, thoughts or ideas. The nod was a nod of defeat, a nod of recognition that he had no hope of bringing his wife home; that for now, she was lost to him. I too felt sick and faint, shaken by what I had witnessed, but knew that I must not think of myself, that I must not let William down.

The walk back to the coach along the same winding streets was desperately difficult. William bit his lip, frowned, murmured to himself abstractly. I tried to think of what I could say, but could only manage, 'You know that Charles and I will give you and the girls aid. You only have to ask, whatever it is you need, William, you know that don't you?'

William nodded and swallowed hard saying, 'You are most kind, Kate, thank you.'

But I did not feel kind at all. I felt hopeless, unable to offer anything more meaningful. Charles was so much better at words than I and I wondered what he would have said if he had been here. Emily was waiting in the carriage and opened her mouth as if to ask how the mistress was, but closed it again after catching sight of William's bloodied face.

On the journey home the shadows of Brompton Asylum troubled me and I pictured Isabella crouched in that dark cell. It was then that the strangest thought occurred to me: I realized that in order to survive her despair Isabella had created about her a world that she could cope with, a world where her daughter was not lost to her at all but lived again among that bundle of rags. In that world death did not exist, did not have the power to hurt nor harm. In that world Isabella was invincible against the cruelty of fate. So would it really be a kindness then to take her from such a benevolent place and bring her back to face reality where only grief and pain were waiting to greet her? Didn't we all to some extent do what Isabella had done? Didn't we all arrange our life in such a way that we perceived it, not as it really was, but as we wished it to be – and in this way we made the hobble of life more bearable? I saw in my mind's eye Isabella's stream of white hair, but when she looked up the face was not hers at all but mine.

Terrified, I quickly brought my mind back into sharp focus, vowing that I would never repeat my thoughts to anyone – lest they think me insane also.

CHAPTER TWENTY-EIGHT

Spring – 1850
St John Street, Clerkenwell

A notice of auction had appeared in *The Times*. The scattered contents of Gore House lay like a dismembered skeleton, its bones now picked bare of flesh by the birds of prey that descended upon it the moment the news was out. Count d'Orsay and the Countess of Blessington were bankrupt; Lord Blessington's estate had been eaten up by debt and Charles had vowed that he would never again venture near the house.

'I could not bear to see that beautiful salon inhabited by slavering hyenas, prowling about and pawing at all my memories. Such wonderful evenings. . . .' he sighed.

I heard that the lovers had crept away under the cover of darkness and escaped to France.

Reversals of fortune, they happened all the time. For the poor, however, I supposed that there was little hope of a reversal of fortune; it seemed that providence decreed that some were destined to go through life with little means, and die in that same condition.

While taking a ride into Town to purchase a new hat I found my thoughts strangely turned in the direction of old Mrs Rozawich. With Isabella in the asylum, I wondered about the old lady and *her* fortune. Had she been befriended by another kindly well-wisher? Was she, indeed, still alive? Moved by the impulse of curiosity, I directed the driver to the old Jewish Quarter.

We turned into Petticoat Lane and the carriage was immediately hindered in its progress by a sea of bearded merchants and their customers. The air was filled with the sound of foreign tongues, shouts and whistles. Washing lines that hung with damp clothing, danced overhead: trousers, shirts, rags without obvious shape or form, all flapping in the wind. Men and women ran alongside the carriage and held up their goods for closer inspection, and I could not help but put a handkerchief to my nose overcome by the odour of rags and old clothes. Realizing that I had set myself a foolish and impossible quest I directed the driver to the synagogue; it seemed the only chance of finding news about the lady I sought, and a remote one at that.

Drawing up outside the place of worship, I wondered what I should do next. Were women permitted to enter and, if so, did they remove their hat, or leave it on? I had no idea of such matters and was beginning to wonder if I was causing myself unnecessary bother, but I resolved to send the driver and bid him to bring the rabbi to the carriage window. I acknowledged that I was so unlike Isabella; her thoughts were always with the needy and those outside of society. I was too caught up in my own concerns to imitate her in this respect, but I would persevere for her sake. If she were ever restored to her senses again, she would feel gladness at this little act of thoughtfulness done in her name.

In a few minutes the driver reappeared with an elderly gentleman, bearded and wearing a long black coat and wide brimmed hat, who I concluded from his appearance, could be no one other than a holy man.

'I understand that you are seeking one of our people, my dear lady.'

I nodded in response.

His blue eyes were set deep in a face so brown and wrinkled that he could have been the patriarch, Abraham, himself.

'We are a vast and numerous population in this fair city. I am

164

not at all sure if I can be of any use to you, but I will try.' He held out his hands in a gesture of humble servitude.

'The lady that I am seeking is named Rozawich.'

The rabbi shook his head slowly. 'There are many by such name, dear lady. Can you tell me anything more?'

I sought the nether regions of my mind; it had been ten years or longer. 'She had an unmarried daughter, Esther, I recall.'

'Again, a name not at all rare for one of our people.'

If only I could remember the name of her son, and then it came in a flash. 'Peter! His name was Peter! Mrs Rozawich was a widow; she had a daughter named Esther, and a son named Peter – he had a second-hand plate and jewellery stall.'

The rabbi hesitated, his blue eyes almost disappearing within the folds of his lids, 'Perhaps… I'm not sure. There is a Peter Rozawich who worked very hard at such a trade and invested his money wisely. He married very well – a widow with property, you could enquire at her address in Clerkenwell.'

I thanked him sincerely and directed the driver to Aylesbury Street, where I enquired at a bank and was able to confirm the address of Mr Peter Rozawich. The carriage turned the corner and pulled up outside a smart three-storey house in St John Street. The driver jumped down and took my card to the door and while I waited, in those few short minutes I realized that I had not reflected at all on what I was going to say, should Old Mrs Rozawich be known here. I also realized that I had not prepared myself to answer questions about Isabella. If old Mrs Rozawich were still to be found in her former condition, it would not be such an awkward matter; however, if she were living here, in much improved circumstances, to refer to the asylum would be indelicate.

I was shortly escorted to the door and shown by a maid to the ornately furnished sitting room, which was occupied by three ladies. The oldest I recognized immediately as Mrs Rozawich, who appeared to be both hale and hearty, but still wearing an expression of grim misgiving upon her lips; the second I remembered as Esther, although somewhat older, and the third was assuredly the young Mrs Rozawich. I was struck by her dark-hair and eyebrows, which framed features of an undoubtedly foreign origin. From her ears hung the most exquisite garnet ear-rings that I had ever seen, and at her throat she wore an opalescent brooch in the form of a butterfly.

We exchanged compliments: I about her jewellery, she about my hat, and then we began polite conversation about my husband's career, as, of course, he was universally known. The young Mrs Rozawich had read many of his novels and had been so keen to receive me when she heard that I was at her door. She enquired into my opinion on all of his compositions, and I was a little ashamed to realize how small an interest I had in such details. His work took up so much of his time and attention, I saw it as something to resent rather than admire.

Old Mrs Rozawich, who had been silently inspecting me very carefully for some time, finally spoke.

'But, Mrs Dickens, whoever would have thought it? Goodness! You have changed. I'm not one to say that a person is overweight, but my, you have grown fat!'

I looked at the faces of the other ladies present with alarm, to see if any shock had registered upon their features, but they raised their gilded cups to their lips in unison and sipped at their tea impassively.

She continued with all sincerity, 'And I'm not one to say that a person has aged; but my, you look so old!'

I watched the garnet ear-rings swinging back and forth from young Mrs Rozawich's ears as she lifted her cup once more to her lips, the tea drinking continuing in quiet synchronization.

When old Mrs Rozawich opened her mouth to say something else, I panicked and looked at Esther, intervening with the first thought that came into my head, 'And you, Esther, are you married now?'

Immediately I knew that it was a clumsy choice of topic, and I coloured up in consequence.

'No, madam, my status is just as it was.'

Esther's response was understandably icy, but any resentment on her part, was no doubt tempered with the satisfaction that if marriage led one to becoming old, fat and clumsy, then she could be glad that she had not entered into such an arrangement.

Young Mrs Rozawich put down her cup and saucer on the side table, and then raised the topic that I was most unprepared for, 'And how is your friend, Mrs Thackeray? I understand that she was very kind to my mother-in-law in days gone by; I trust that she is in good health?'

I was pleased to manage a more polished response than I had hoped for. 'I am afraid to say, that she is not, madam, but I will let her know of your family's good wishes for her prompt return to health.'

My evasive reply indicated that no further questions should be asked, if a person did not want to appear impertinent, and thankfully old Mrs Rozawich was sensitive to it. Perhaps she had the remains of some loyalty to her friend after all.

Upon climbing into the carriage to make my return home, I noticed that the doorway seemed narrower than when we had arrived and I feared that I would become wedged in it! Strangely, my body ached with pains that I had not been aware of before, no doubt about it, I was getting older; and when I observed the hands that were folded in my ample lap, the truth was plain to see: they were undeniably plump. So much for charitable acts!

CHAPTER TWENTY-NINE

March 1851
Russell Square, Bloomsbury

The room was comfortable, given an air of cosiness by the well-tended fire in the grate. On either side of the fireplace were fitted cupboards: one stacked with china, the other in use as a bookcase. A large sash window framed by white cotton curtains overlooked the little front garden and, seated by the fire, his feet resting on a plain but highly polished fender, was my father-in-law. His legs were wrapped in a woollen blanket, and his large thick hands grasped at the folds at regular intervals as pain flooded through his ageing body.

'I ain't afraid of a-dying, Kate, I'll just be glad to get rid of this 'ere pain in me kidneys; and when I gets back on me feet again, I'll take the 'ole bloomin' family out to the tea gardens – my treat, mind, I won't have my son puttin' his hand in 'is pocket for me – and we'll play skittles, and watch the fireworks light up the 'ole sky.'

At this Mr Dickens closed his eyes as another surge of pain overwhelmed him and he clawed at the folds in the blanket again. Seated at his side on a low, padded footstool, I placed my hand upon his. He opened his eyes again as the pain subsided, and smiled his usual optimistic smile, as if he were sure that the passing spasm was the last.

John Dickens's history was not in any way a remarkable one

for his time. All that had been notable about my father-in-law was that in this unforgiving life he had survived – perhaps not nobly, but he had survived. As a young man an inheritance of £450 had slipped unnoticed through his prodigal fingers; he could never in any precise manner recall when or how it had happened, but it had happened, all the same. He had not been troubled by it, though, and had spent the remainder of his adult life convinced that good fortune was once again awaiting him around the proverbial corner.

If thoughts of meeting his Maker now crossed his mind, he undoubtedly had many a ready excuse as to why he had put a young boy to work in a blacking factory to pay off his own debts, forged the signature of that very same son to raise a pound or two, and unashamedly begged from his offspring's highly esteemed friends.

My father-in-law looked wistfully out of the window.

'Tell the guvnor I asked after 'im and that 'is old Pa knows that 'e's a-busy makin' 'is way in the world. Even though 'e don't say much, 'e cares. I know 'e cares, Kate.'

'Of course he does, Pa.' I patted his hand reassuringly, and he grasped at it suddenly, squeezing it so tightly that I wanted to shout out in pain too.

'There, there now, Mr Dickens; no more talking, you must save your energy for the operation.'

Mrs Davey's soft voice betrayed no hint of the torturous ordeal that my father-in-law was about to endure, but was full of the calm reassurance that was reflected in her motherly face. I was unsure as to whether in fact she was indeed a mother, the house seemed tolerably quiet and well suited to the needs of two people grown weary of the world outside, so I concluded that she must in fact be childless. But I was convinced that the tender care she would by nature have heaped upon such children, was instead directed to those she now nursed in a different manner.

Charles's parents had been taken into the home of Mrs Davey and her husband, a surgeon at the hospital in Whitechapel Road, and Charles was reassured that his increasingly forgetful mother would be watched so as not to take off in the middle of the night, and that his father would have all of his ailments attended to by a qualified doctor.

My husband had always found it an uncomfortable obligation to visit his parents, being either uncharacteristically tongue-tied or impatiently censorious with them both. He had never really forgiven them for being who they were, and he always placed responsibility for any demons that he had faced in his adult life at their feet. If he was an impatient, sensitive man who wrestled with anxiety, that was his mother's fault; if he had a morbid fear of being in debt, then that was his father's fault. But at the terrifying thought that he might lose his father for good, he had gone about his morning business as if nothing at all untoward were about to take place that day. It was the only way that he knew how to manage such dire apprehension.

Mrs Dickens sat at the other side of the fire in an easy chair. A small dog sat curled upon her lap, preoccupied with an invisible insect upon its hind leg at which it gnawed with determination.

Mrs Dickens stared at me without an ounce of recognition in her eyes.

'Are you the new maid?' she asked suspiciously.

'No, 'tis I, madam, Kate.'

Still she stared at me blankly.

'You are too stout to be the maid – the cook then?' She reached out a bent finger with which to poke me, and I drew back with uncertainty. I had always been rather wary of my mother-in-law and, in her present state of mind, I could not be sure of her next move.

'No, madam, I am your daughter-in-law, Charles's wife.'

'Charles?'

'Yes, your son, madam.'

Her eyes opened wide as if suddenly she saw everything clearly and her expression changed to one of revulsion.

'Charles!' She spat out the name with contempt. 'That ungrateful child, always did have ideas above his station. Thought a deal too much of himself, that boy, shutting us away here as if he is ashamed of us!'

Quick to defend my husband, I moved towards her and placed my hand on hers in all earnestness, completely forgetting my earlier caution, 'No, madam, he has placed you here with good people, people who will care for your every need.'

At the feel of my skin upon hers, she withdrew sharply as though she had been touched by something unholy, and slapped my hand smartly.

'Lizzie, Lizzie,' her husband soothed, 'the girl meant no harm. . . .' At another surge of pain, his voice trailed off.

The rebuke stung more than just physically. The room was hot and the thought of the terrible operation that my father-in-law was about to endure made me feel distressed and nauseous, and where was Charles in the midst of all of this? He should have been here at my side supporting me, supporting his father, not hiding his head in an imaginary world. When I had hinted that morning that he should visit his father, lest everything not turn out as expected, he had snapped, 'The surgeon is being handsomely paid to perform well, and I expect him to do it!' It was as though by holding such an expectation, providence could bring about only one acceptable outcome and no other!

Mrs Davey sensed my state of heightened emotion and gently ushered me out of the room. If she spoke, I had no comprehension of it for all I could hear was the fading torrent of a ceaseless monologue coming from the sitting room.

'That boy could have been manager of that blacking factory by now, John Dickens, if I'd have had my way. But no, you had to interfere, putting ideas in his head. Books! That was the root of it all, giving him all those books to read as a child. Filled his head with ideas of grandeur, ideas above his station. Where did books ever get you, John Dickens? Aye, you've had your name down in a book, many a time, a debt-collector's book . . . shutting us away here. . . .'

Her ranting faded as I became aware of Mrs Davey's words. 'As soon as there is any news, madam, I will let you know. Your father-in-law will be in good hands, do not worry.'

Her kindly manner momentarily disarmed me, and I wanted

to throw myself into those motherly arms of hers and sob, but for the sake of propriety, I simply thanked her politely and replied that I would convey to my husband that she was carrying out her duties just as he had directed. Mrs Davey nodded her head, but looked upon me with sympathetic eyes as I stepped into the carriage to leave. She had not been fooled.

John Dickens never again visited the tea gardens, played skittles or watched the fireworks light up the night sky. Charles had gone to his mother as soon as he had received the news and promised her that she would never be without his assistance, but she had remained silent, looking past him as if he did not exist. He did not come home that night but walked aimlessly, wandering through dark and joyless alleyways until he came to a place that made sense of his loss and despair. A few coins had secured him a place to sleep, and if the guard had been surprised by the request he had not shown it.

Forster called the following morning and with some difficulty explained my husband's whereabouts.

'Perhaps, Kate, you might be able to persuade him to leave. I have done my best, you know, but a woman's sympathetic manner of speaking and all that. . . .' He cleared his throat as if I knew exactly what 'all that' was supposed to mean and how it was to be employed in encouraging a grieving man to leave a police cell.

'If you cannot persuade him to come home, John, then I do not see what I can do that will make any difference. But I will come, none the less.'

The tiny room was dark and although my husband was quite free to leave, he had chosen to keep the door firmly shut. I entered with Forster at my side and as my eyes adjusted to the darkness, his face emerged from it and I saw him seated upon a mattress of straw.

'Have you come to take me home, Kate?'

His voice was weary through lack of sleep.

'*Home*,' he sighed. 'Now there's a word. But what does it mean: home?'

Forster looked at me and whispered, 'He's been acting this way since I saw him last.'

'If home is where the heart is, then my home is right here, Kate, here among people who know what it is to have lost everything.'

He got up from the straw mattress and walked to the barred window that overlooked a courtyard and stared out into it.

'Do you know, it's a strange twist of irony, but all of my life I was waiting for my father to tell me that he was proud of me, proud to call me his own. But I did not realize until now that my father was waiting too – waiting to hear the very same words from his son. And now he will never. . . .'

CHAPTER THIRTY

1851
Malvern

My Dearest Kate
I hope that you are feeling in somewhat better spirits than when I
left you. My story is shaping up well, but now I am faced with the
dilemma of what to do with poor Dora. Should I kill her or
not. . . ?

Abruptly I stopped reading, shocked by my husband's insensitivity. With our own little Dora still so little, it seemed an ill-chosen name for a character so undoubtedly fated to die.

I thought about my baby daughter and how much I missed her. Yet, in spite of this, I did not feel ready to return to the responsibilities of motherhood. I had nine children waiting at home for me, but the death of Charles's father had been most unsettling. The stay in Malvern had done me good, the quiet surroundings of the countryside had helped to soothe my troubled nerves. Georgie was surely doing a fine job and knowing that the children were being cared for with the utmost dedication was a great comfort. In fact, I often wondered if I was being missed at all.

Charles had written regularly and had visited twice, staying for as long as his busy schedule had allowed, and I looked forward to his correspondence. For Charles, writing was as natural as breathing and I felt as though I enjoyed more of his company in this way than I did when I was in his presence. His thoughts and feelings were all routinely recorded and it often felt as though he were here in this very room. I laughed at the accounts of his daily comings and goings and his lively descriptions of the children's antics, and bristled up a little with resentment at his frequent references to Georgie's 'capital efficiency'.

The following day I received yet another letter bearing Charles's handwriting and I wondered what could have happened to cause him to write again so soon. More words of deserved praise for Georgie, no doubt! I sat down, sipping at my tea and began to read:

My Dearest Kate

Since writing to you last, sickness has visited our home in the most unexpected way. I know that you are not strong and cannot bear any further distress at this time. However, if I were not to prepare you, I am convinced that your suffering would be greater.

Our little Dora has been taken very ill and at present Doctor Bell is unable to find the cause of the trouble. Georgie, as you would expect is making a first class nurse and never leaves the baby's side for a moment. However, we cannot and should not expect Providence to look upon our family with any more favour than it does others. So if I should have to write to you again and tell you that our little daughter has been taken from us, you must be strong and bear it with all the dignity that you can summon. Please don't fail me in this, Kate. Remember, you must be strong. . . !

I held the letter – momentarily paralysed – then folded it and quickly replaced it in its envelope as if it were hidden then it could not really exist, nor have any power to harm. I swallowed hard in an effort to quell the rising hysteria. 'Now, Catherine,' I said to myself, 'what would Charles say if he were here? Would he not say: *all will be well if only we stay strong?* Didn't he say the very same thing when Charley was ill? He was right on that occasion. . . . So why should that not be the case now?'

I felt a little calmer and decided that I must return home immediately, but did not send word of my coming lest Charles should forbid it. I took out my travelling bag and began to pack. But, despite repeated searching, I could only find one of my best travelling shoes and no matter how hard I looked I could not find the other. It was the same with my gloves; one plum coloured gauntlet lay on its own upon the bed. I searched through the drawers of the dressing table, scrutinized the empty wardrobe and carefully examined beneath the bed until I could no longer keep up the pretence of fortitude and my despair finally took hold of me. It was no good. I was not like Charles and never could be. Life was all too real for me and I knew only too well that it could be hard and cruel, no matter how hard we willed it not to be.

Upon hearing my sobs the landlady quietly knocked the door and, seeing my distress told me not to mind, she would see to the packing and would call for the cab to take me home. In her fifty or sixty years, she had no doubt aided many a tearful young woman who had come to Malvern to rest a disquieted mind, and she was not perturbed.

The journey back to London seemed interminable. I longed to return home to my little Dora, to hold her in my arms and put my hand upon her brow. The coach was crowded and I was squashed between a parson and his over-fed wife who munched on a succession of rations fetched from a basket on her lap, while her husband slept, occasionally dropping his head upon my shoulder and immediately waking with an earnest apology. Opposite sat two ladies and an elderly gentleman whom I soon learned was their brother. The sisters, as far as I could discern, were not twins and yet they seemed so very much of one mind that I nicknamed them 'Harriet and Henrietta'. Whatever the one began to say, the other would finish or repeat for emphasis.

'Our brother, Mr Allen, used to—'

'—be a soldier,' the other concluded.

Mr Allen nodded, but did not speak.

'He was part of a regiment that fought long and hard—'

'—at the Battle of Waterloo.'

'Yes, the Battle of Waterloo,' the first echoed.

The mute Mr Allen nodded agreeably once more. I did not know if he could not speak, or had given up trying through the lack of opportunity, but he did not need to say a single word during the entire journey, for it was all said quite ably on his behalf.

When my carriage finally pulled up, I realized that the relentless conversation had passed the time admirably well, but had left me exhausted. My head was throbbing.

'I hope—'

'—that your little daughter is soon well again.'

'Soon well. Yes,' they chorused together.

Mr Allen gave a mute nod and waved me goodbye.

As soon as I opened the front door I sensed the presence of despair. I ran up the stairs, stumbling and calling, 'Georgie! Dora! Where are you?'

I heard the click of the bedroom door and, on reaching the top of the stairs, saw Charles standing guard. He wore an expression of graveness upon his face.

'We were not expecting you, Kate. You should not have come.'

'Where is she?' I insisted. 'I want to see her.'

'I'm sorry, Kate.' He shook his head.

I removed my bonnet and gloves. 'You can tell her that her mama is here now. That I have come home to help her get better.'

My voice wavered, full of unease.

I placed my hand upon the doorknob and Charles covered it with his own and prevented me from turning it.

'You must not go in, Kate.' He tried to mask his emotion with authority. 'She has already gone, has been gone for two days. It is best if you don't—'

As his words took on meaning, my knees gave way and I dropped at his feet.

'But why didn't you tell me? Why did you let me believe. . . ? Oh, dear God, let me see her, Charles. Please! You must. You must.'

He helped me up and led me to the bedroom where he put me to bed and brought me brandy to aid my rest, leaving Emily to watch at my bedside.

Dora's funeral took place the following morning, but I could not attend, still suffering from the disclosure of her death only the day before. Despite determined efforts to raise myself and get dressed, my mind could not command what my body could not manage. Charles was very kind and reassured me that it was quite in order for me to stay at home and that he thought it best under the circumstances. I watched from the bedroom window as Georgie took his arm and climbed into the carriage.

Suddenly my mind, which until now had been numbed by shock, became quite clear and focused upon a horrifying thought: had Georgie really done all that she could to prevent the death of my dear Dora? Had she formed a scheme to ingratiate herself further with Charles? Yes! Now I saw it all so clearly. She had had me sent away to Malvern so as to part me from Charles. She had let my baby die and then planned to be the only one there to comfort him when it happened. I banged my fist upon the window and repeatedly called to my husband, shouting his name. When at last he looked up, his eyes were full of sadness and pain. He stepped into the carriage, which pulled away and headed for the cemetery. Dora had gone and I could hardly believe it.

CHAPTER THIRTY-ONE

July 1853
Tavistock House, London

'These doors here, I want them to be folding, like so. Then I can walk between my study and the drawing room; pace up and down, you know, when I'm thinking.'

The builders had taken over the house: Charles had thought that a change of accommodation would help us all to put the past behind us, and so in 1851 we left Devonshire Terrace and moved down to Tavistock Square. I liked the house well enough, although there was much to be done in the way of decoration and repair, but I did not feel that I belonged here, or was mistress of the house at all. Georgie was increasing her authority week by week.

'What do you think, my dear, should the recess here in the drawing room be turned into a cupboard or a bookcase?' Charles asked Georgie, hooking his thumbs into his waistcoat pocket.

Young Francis held up his schoolwork for my sister to inspect, she nodded briskly with approval and then turned her attention back to Charles.

'A bookcase, Charles, that is what is needed. If the drawing room is to adjoin your study, then you will have the extra storage you require for your books close at hand.'

His face lit up at her suggestion, 'Capital! Georgie, Captital! You are right as usual.'

'P-P-papa?' Francis stammered, and held out his school book to Charles, in search of commendation.

Charles ruffled his hair, 'What have we here, then, young man? Let me see.'

'It is a m-m-map of the world, P-Papa, I have d-drawn it.'

Charles crouched down on his haunches, with all seriousness upon his face.

'My dear fellow, geography is all very well, but we cannot have stuttering in the Dickens family. You must try to conquer it, Francis, or people will think you a fool.'

'Yes, P-Papa.'

With an air of dejection, Francis left the room and I followed close behind.

'Do not become down-hearted, my love, we are all different and unique. You have a genuine talent for drawing, you know, such an eye for detail.'

He lifted his boyish face and smiled. 'Do you really think so, M-Mama?'

'I am sure of it, my love.'

I sighed as he raced away up the stairs, cheered by my words. Charles had such high expectations for his sons, but how could they even begin to emulate their father's achievements? I worried for them.

Upon returning to the drawing room I found Charles asking Georgie for her opinion on the curtains and the carpets. I hovered in the doorway for a moment, unsure of what to do and then turned back into the hall again; it was obvious that I was not needed.

August 1853

As the summer passed I noticed that Charles's circle of friends was evolving and changing, and I was sorry to see that my husband was becoming increasingly irritated by Forster. They often had their arguments, which had characterized the entire lifetime of their friendship, but of late Charles spoke of his old friend in the most disparaging terms.

'The man bores me, Kate; he has become an old stick-in-the-mud since he married, and he is always interfering in my affairs.'

'But you know, dear, that he only has your best interests at heart.'

'Can you believe it, Kate, he had the audacity to suggest that I should not lower myself to the public reading of my books? It is the most marvellous way to make money and yet the man says with greatest presumption, "*It's just not done, old fellow. People will think you nothing more than a strolling player; and, of course you are so much more than that!*" Pompous windbag! What does he know of such matters? Does he think that I can run a house of this size on nothing?'

Charles peered closely into the looking-glass above the sitting-room fireplace and with practised care positioned a stray curl over his receding hairline.

'And Macready: he is nearly sixty now. Oh, don't misunderstand me, Kate, he is a legendary performer and I have the greatest admiration for him, but I need to surround myself with men of my own age. After all I am still a young man!'

After completing his self-admiration in the glass, he began to tell me of an intriguing young author he had met by the name of Wilkie Collins.

'The fellow has nothing excessively formal about him, Kate – spirited little chap, I like him!'

Charles then pulled at his cravat, loosening it a little, as if there was something uncomfortable he wanted to say, that would not pass beyond the knot.

'I was thinking of going on a tour of Italy, with him actually, and taking Augustus Egg, along too. Collins and I can use the time to write, and Egg will enjoy painting the scenery, so we will all benefit in one way or another.'

He shot me a quick glance to estimate my response and then continued, 'It will be a working holiday, of course, my dear, that is what I am trying to say.'

Before I had any chance to comment, he looked at his pocket watch, remarked that he must get on with his work, and made a swift exit to his study.

Mr Collins was a strange looking fellow, of short stature and with a head that seemed disproportionate in size. Upon meeting him he did not appear to be the same person that Charles had spoken of at all. In fact, I found him rather serious-minded and appearing to observe everything that was said and done with the closest attention. When he shook me by the hand I felt that he was looking right into my very soul.

One evening, when Charles had invited his new friends to supper, amidst the sound of laughter and the clink of cutlery, I noticed through the French windows that someone appeared to be hiding in the bushes. I did not want to alert Charles to it for when my old worries came upon me, I often imagined things; so I excused myself from the table with the intention of making sure of what I had seen. I quietly stepped out into the garden and found that it was no fancy of my imagination at all, for there amongst the foliage was my brother-in-law, Fred.

His appearance was quite alarming: he had lost weight, his face was pale and drawn, and he had the most terrible cough.

'Fred, what in the world has happened to you? Don't stand out here, you will catch your death. Come in the house and join us for dinner.'

He remained fixed to the spot and shook his head resolutely.

'Come, Fred, we must be able to do something for you, just tell me what you need and it's yours.'

Fred snorted with derision, 'Ah, that's right, Kate, *young Frederick* couldn't be here without wanting something, now, could he?'

He began to cough violently again and I took his arm to lead him into the house, and this time he did not resist. I sat him down in Charles's study and rang for Cook to bring him something to eat and drink.

He gulped thirstily at the ale that was in a short while handed to him and then started on the beef stew, its heat hardly seeming to burn his mouth at all, so great was his hunger.

'*Kate! Where in God's name have you got to?*'

I heard Charles's footsteps outside in the hall and urged Cook to run and tell him that I was seeing to one of the children, and would be back directly.

Fred rose unsteadily to his feet. 'I had better go, Kate. There will only be a row if he finds me here, especially in his study.'

'But you must tell me what has become of you. Where is your wife?'

Fred had broken off the engagement to his fiancée and married her sister instead. His father-in-law had cut them off without a penny and they had existed entirely on his earnings from his job in the Treasury.

'We've been arguing again, Kate. I have lost my job; I took some money from my employer – I intended to pay it back, in truth I did – but they found out before I had the chance and I. . . .'

He doubled up with another fit of coughing which gave me great cause for concern, but I had no money of my own to give him for a doctor, and I did not dare to search through Charles's desk. While Cook put together a small sack of provisions for him to take away, Fred wrote out his address and I noticed how he struggled to control the strokes of the pen. He looked up at me wearily.

'Without even trying, I have turned out to be my father's son, Kate, haven't I?' His voice conveyed a sense of hopelessness that cut deep to my heart.

'When the moment is right, Fred, I will speak to your brother. For all of his faults, he would not want to see you this way.'

I wished him well and watched his weary figure leave through the gate and I wondered, what had happened to that self-assured young boy whom I had known in days gone by?

When I returned to the dining room, the guests were drinking coffee and I noticed that Mr Collins was endeavouring to pour into his cup with discretion, a few drops of potion from a small phial. My unexpected entrance appeared to have unnerved him and he sprinkled the liquid all over the tablecloth. He turned a bright shade of crimson and I was unsure as to whether he was afflicted by rage or shame.

'No matter, no matter,' he spluttered, blotting the cloth with his napkin. 'I have neuralgia, madam, very painful it is indeed.' He examined the remaining contents of the phial, peering at it closely through his thick-lensed glasses, and realizing that it was almost empty, he became noticeably afflicted with worry. Beads of perspiration broke out upon his rounded forehead, he stood up abruptly and made his excuses to leave. I began to feel a strange sense of unease over the habits of my husband's new acquaintance.

CHAPTER THIRTY-TWO

1855
Carter Lane, Ludgate Hill

I sat in the morning room, leafing through bills and trying to audit the housekeeping books. Numbers, letters, symbols jumped around before my eyes, switching places no matter how I tried to pinpoint them with a stab of the pen. Georgie and I had had a heated exchange of words in the kitchen that morning and poor Cook had not known which way to pass the books.

'Am I not mistress in this house, Georgie?'

'Yes, of course, dear, but Charles has said—'

'*Charles* has a wife! And as long as that fact remains then I will oversee such household duties as I have always done.'

Why didn't that woman leave my husband out of matters and go and find a husband of her own?

The morning-room door flew open, 'Kate! Am I to understand that you are in possession of the housekeeping books?' Charles's voice was full of irritation.

His eyes fell upon the green-bound records and I instinctively put my hands over the pages, covering the blots and crossings out that I had inevitably made.

'How many times must I tell you to leave such matters to Georgie? The last time you meddled with those books it took me hours to sort it out, and I really don't have the time for such things.'

'Meddle? I'm not meddling, Charles, but how am I supposed to run this house if I am not even permitted—?'

'Kate, if I ever catch you—' He thumped his fist upon the table. 'Just leave well alone, before you drive me insane with frustration.'

In his display of anger he had dropped the morning post which he had held in his hand, and he crouched down and picked up the letters one by one, until he came to the last one, which he looked at with uncertainty. He stood up and turned it over before speaking.

'Kate,' he sighed, 'I think that I had better tell you that I have been corresponding with Maria Beadnell for some little while.'

I stiffened at the mention of her name, even now it stirred up strong emotions.

'Now, I do not consider myself obliged to inform you' – he had begun to pace the room, his hands behind his back – 'but in view of your past feelings in connection with Maria, I think it best to tell you. It appears that life has not been kind to her recently and although she has not revealed the full nature of her misfortune, I would like to offer a listening ear to an old family friend.'

A look of displeasure crossed my face. '*An old family friend! That she has never been.*'

Charles did not notice; engrossed in his own saintliness he continued to chide me. 'So, should you see a letter arrive for me written in her hand, you will not come looking for me with accusations, will you?'

I was not too old to blush at the reminder of an embarrassing episode in my life and I felt belittled by his condescending words. My husband had a marvellous way of manoeuvring matters so that his own weaknesses were obscured by highlighting the failings of others.

'Very well,' I demurred, smoothing down my skirts. 'I am grateful that you have told me.'

'Then it's all agreed, we will call upon Mrs Winter tomorrow.'

'Call on her? Charles. . . !' But before I could object to his ridiculous suggestion, he had left the room and I found that I was quivering with anger and astonishment. How did he expect me to endure such an insufferable introduction?'

Maria Beadnell had long since become Mrs Henry Winter. Her husband was a handsome, well-educated businessman, but his fortune had long since dwindled and he now found himself in the employ of a gambling house. He enticed the players to raise the stakes, cheered with those who won and encouraged those who lost that their luck was guaranteed to change with the next game. Well-dressed gentleman played roulette alongside tradesmen, money-lenders or lawyers. There was no prejudice about where a man's money came from, all that mattered was that he had sufficient funds to play. From time to time there would be a sharp whistle from outside, followed by an impromptu police raid, but more often than not all that would be found were the well-rehearsed moves of gentlemen eating from a cold buffet, smoking cigars and drinking sherry. By day, Henry Winter continued the charade of a profession in the City and thus his wife remained oblivious to his nocturnal occupation, or so he had thought.

The following morning I awoke with the hazy sensation that something unpleasant had happened the day before and then I remembered Charles's words: *'We will call upon Mrs Winter tomorrow.'*

Charles was already dressed and had made his daily circuit of Camden before breakfast. Upon meeting on the landing he did not attempt to engage me in conversation and I was glad of it, for I had not the heart for a pretence at cordiality. The journey by carriage to Ludgate Hill was similarly wordless, until we arrived at Carter Lane. Without making eye contact Charles instructed, 'Now I expect you to be polite to Maria, Kate, and you must under no circumstances, embarrass me, is that understood?' He then set about adjusting his cravat, smoothing down his hair and buttoning up his jacket.

Maria occupied a town house that was distinguished from its

neighbours by its neglected exterior and faded grandeur. The paint on the door was peeling, thick layers of soot blackened the windows, and the steps were spattered with the mud thrown up by the passing carts. Charles, who was a martinet for order, did not say one word about it and I wondered what we were about to discover inside. We were shown in by a butler whose suit appeared to have belonged to a long-serving predecessor, and one who had been a good deal shorter at that. Occasionally giving each of his cuffs a self-conscious tug, he escorted us to the sparsely furnished sitting room where an odd assortment of chairs formed a semi-circular arrangement around an aged piano; and we gave them a necessary flick with a handkerchief before sitting down. What a strange reception!

Above the fireplace hung a portrait of the young Maria. I could see that Charles was mesmerized by it as he took in each long-remembered feature; and when he caught my eye, he blushed like an awkward youth. As a whole the portrait was one of youthful innocence and beauty, but upon closer examination there was an air of caprice in the eyes, a haughtiness about the nose and a look of beguile in her sweet smile. Perhaps Charles imagined that the years had made no impression on those girlish features, or the mane of dark hair – he certainly did not see his own receding hair line or frown lines. I am sure that he saw himself as the curly haired boy who had once been completely smitten by Miss Maria Beadnell, so he was not at all prepared for the portly, middle-aged woman who entered the room with a slight sway in her step.

'My dearest Charles,' she gushed, fluttering her eyelashes, 'you have not changed at all.'

Charles opened his mouth and closed it again realizing that he could not return the compliment.

'And you look ... well too, my dear Mrs Winter.' His eyes took in her over-rouged cheeks and ill-fitting wig; he dared not look at her smile lest she be missing any teeth.

'Please, call me Maria, let us not be formal with each other. After all, do you not remember the letters you wrote me? Twice a day sometimes, I recall.' She leaned forward and fluttered her eyelashes again and giggled. The sight of this middle-aged woman making love to him was too much for Charles and he pulled at his collar, and took out his handkerchief to mop his top lip.

This was making the journey entirely worthwhile and I was greatly enjoying myself, but I came to his rescue anyway. 'How long are you in London, Mrs Winter?'

'Until my husband has run up debts and enemies enough to warrant our hasty departure,' Maria brayed, without a trace of embarrassment. 'He thinks that I do not know where he goes at night. He thinks that I am a fool.' She turned to Charles. 'Do you think me a fool, Charles?'

He opened his mouth but no words came out and I came to his rescue again, this time with a change of topic.

'And have you children, ma'am?'

At this her expression changed to one of sadness. 'Alas, Mr Winter and I were not blessed in that way, 'tis a pity, but there it is,' she sighed. 'P'raps it's as well in light of our financial circumstances,' and her eyes fell upon Charles.

I could almost hear my husband's thoughts of alarm as I witnessed the horror creeping across his face: *She has mentioned money again! Is that why she has brought me here, to ask for my assistance?*

Maria stood up, gave her wig a self-conscious pat and, after glancing with disappointment at an empty decanter, she secured her uncertain gait by holding on to the back of each chair she passed until she arrived at the piano and sat down at it. She began to sing in a very shrill soprano and I was unsure as to whether to laugh or cry with pity. Charles held his handkerchief to his mouth and winced at each piercing note, and as she at last came to a piercing finale, he stood up rapidly and shook her hand with great haste, saying that he had pressing business in the City and must really bid her goodbye.

'So soon? But we had so much more to talk about. Shall I see you again?'

But Charles did not answer, only slammed the carriage door behind him. Maria stood in the doorway waving her lace handkerchief and calling, 'Do come again, won't you, Charles? I have so many friends who would relish an introduction.'

I never thought that I would have cause to pity one of whom I had once been so jealous, but I wished that providence would look upon Maria with greater kindness in the future.

CHAPTER THIRTY-THREE

July 1857
Brompton Asylum, London

Isabella sat looking out at the terraced gardens of the asylum. Her white hair, which at one time she would allow no one to touch, was now neatly tied up in a pleat. Dressed in a brown woollen day-dress with a clean white apron over the top, I was glad to see that the stained dress that she had been clothed in since her arrival and the eyeless doll that she had clung to, were thankfully no more. Despite Isabella's long absence, William had been a wonderful father to his two daughters. He had employed a governess for them and they had recently been introduced into society as accomplished young ladies, who were well travelled, fluent in both French and Italian and knowledgeable about all of the arts.

William, I suspected, was not looking after himself at all though. His curly hair had greyed, and his face had taken on an air of permanent dejection. Plagued by a recurring kidney infection, he had made matters worse by over-eating and heavy-drinking, and I thought how sad it was that Isabella was completely unaware of her husband's success as an author, for the height of his fame had come during her absence. Now William worried repeatedly that he was losing his ability to write, and had been so lonely without Isabella at his side, that he had found solace in an innocent correspondence with the wife of an old friend from his days at Cambridge; but when her husband had found the letters, he was enraged with misplaced jealousy and forbade any future contact between the two.

In spite of his loneliness, William continued to be a loyal and faithful husband and visited Isabella regularly, and I admired him greatly. He had done all that he could to secure her comfort; she had been moved some time ago to the east wing of the asylum where the screams and shouts of the west wing could only be heard when the wind changed direction. A set of French windows opened out from her room, and led out onto a paved terrace that sloped down gently to well-tended gardens. Sitting at her side, I quietly observed three of the patients assisting the gardener, hoeing out weeds and pulling up vegetables from the vegetable patch. I felt strangely at ease here looking out at the view and in Isabella's silent company, somehow feeling that I could be entirely myself with her. She had no expectations, no demands; she accepted my presence on whatever terms it came, and I found it a comfort to bask in that acceptance.

It was never easy to speak on the subject I had in my mind, but I felt the need to unburden my soul to someone and I steeled myself to say the words.

'I don't know if William has ever felt able to share my sadness with you, and I have not mentioned it on my previous visits, Izzy, but now you seem a little better, I feel that I can tell you, for I feel that you of all people will understand. I lost my little Dora, my little girl. She was just an infant, not much younger than your Jane was when she. . . .'

Isabella did not flinch at the sound of the name of her own lost child, but continued to gaze in peaceful contemplation at the garden.

'It has been six years now, but it is all as fresh in my mind as if it were only yesterday. Even now, I cannot help but think that if only I'd been at home, then perhaps there would have been a different outcome. I feel so guilty that I wasn't there to nurse her and that maybe I could have done something. And no matter how much I go over it in my mind, I can't believe that she has gone, Izzy, and I wonder if I ever will.'

Isabella did not avert her eyes from the view but very slowly lifted her hand from her lap, and her fingers crept out and intertwined with my own. My throat tightened with sadness.

'I try to talk to Charles about her, but he won't entertain the subject. It's as if a part of him has closed off to it, as if it never happened. But I feel that if I don't talk about her then I shall go— That is, my heart will break.'

I looked down at my wedding ring and sighed. My heart was so full of unspoken hopelessness.

'It's not just that Charles shuts me out when I try to talk about Dora, but when I try to reach him on any subject other than the trivialities of life, he appears uninterested. Oh yes, he will talk about Forster, Mr Collins, Miss Burdett-Coutts and his work at the home for fallen women. He will talk about the menu for dinner on Sunday, or whom we should invite to join us for an evening at the theatre. But mostly he just looks right through me when he talks as if I was not a person whose name he knows, but simply a figure who needs to be addressed out of necessity from time to time.'

Isabella's fingers tightened around my own.

'I can sense that I irritate him with unbearable frustration, but he always stops short of voicing it. Sometimes he can be kind, mostly when he has been impatient with me and feels some sense of guilt, but yesterday he did the strangest thing, he unexpectedly gave me a posy of flowers. I confess that I was completely wrong-footed, and didn't know what to say at all. He even noticed what I was wearing and complimented me on it. But although he was looking right at me, it was as if he was imposing someone else in my place, as if it wasn't me he was courting at all. I can't explain it, Izzy, it was quite perplexing.'

A nurse passed us by, acknowledging Isabella with a kindly nod and entered the infirmary through the French windows.

'I know now that whatever show of happiness Charles presents to others, that deep down he is truly unhappy. When we came home from Europe last month he argued furiously with my parents over the state in which they had left the house, and Mama has vowed never to set foot in the house again. Then, last month, we held a party at home to celebrate the success of Charles's latest theatrical performance with Mr Collins. As usual he was the life and soul once the guests arrived, and made great jokes with Mr Collins that he should under no circumstances smoke his cigars in the study lest he set it on fire, but an hour before he was as morose as I've ever seen him. He sat on the end of the bed, sulking, and when I asked what was wrong, he said, *"Tell me, Kate, what have I done with my life that has any meaning?"*

'I told him that he had his work to be proud of and that people worshipped him wherever he went; but he shrugged it off, saying, "It's just words, Kate, that is all I am known for, words."

' "But they are very clever words, my love".' I reassured him, "I could not write as you do".'

'Then young Charley tapped on the door to wish his Papa congratulations, but instead of receiving his son's good wishes, he lectured the poor young man on how he should be applying himself better to his career and berated him for having no ambition, no drive, no enthusiasm; and then he turned to me with a look as if to say that I was somehow to blame!'

One of the male patients who had been assisting the gardener, came to the foot of the terraced steps and began to lay out in a most precise manner, each of the vegetables he had pulled up. He began with an exact row of carrots, then below that a row of potatoes. He continued with the lettuces and radishes until finally he set out a row of onions, before turning and running back to his employment at the gardener's side.

'Looking at this beautiful garden here, reminds me of the new house that Charles has purchased at Gad's Hill,' I went on. 'It is in such a tranquil setting, Izzy, you would love it there. He says that he plans to use it as a country retreat, but I have only seen it once as for some reason he seems reluctant to take me there again. It's as if I do not have a place there at all. You know what, Izzy, I somehow feel that I never will.'

Isabella gently lifted her fingers from mine, slowly stood up and began to walk down the terraced steps towards the lawns, humming to herself, and I followed her, realizing that I had been ceaseless in the outpouring of my troubles.

'I'm so sorry, dear,' I sighed, 'I have been entirely selfish in talking only of my own concerns. Forgive me – is there anything that I can do for you?'

'Yes.' She spoke unexpectedly and turned to me with the greatest recognition that I had seen in her eyes for a long while. 'Yes, there is.'

There was a measured deliberateness in her voice. 'I . . . want . . . to go back home.'

His cuffs were still worn and threadbare, his sleeves still turned back, a sign of his enduring readiness to employ himself to the needs of his patients. The lines on his brow had deepened, and the eyes behind his spectacles dimmed. Doctor Hargreaves had been here long before Isabella's arrival and he was here still.

'But she is so much better, Doctor, you must have seen it yourself? I cannot understand why you won't consider allowing her to return home.'

Doctor Hargreaves looked out of his study window across to the gardens where Isabella walked in apparent contentment.

'She has no other home now, she has been here so long that she knows nothing else, despite what you might think. Outside these walls is a world that will be so strange and terrifying to her that the recovery that has taken so long to effect, could be undone in a moment. Nothing could prepare her for such a sudden change of circumstances. Believe me, madam, we would be doing her no kindness whatsoever if we exposed her to such a fate.'

'But she has asked to go home; you cannot be so hard-hearted as to ignore that, sir? Surely she must remember something of her home in order to make such a request?'

Doctor Hargreaves smiled at my over-simplification of matters – matters that he knew to be far more complex.

'Think back, madam; perhaps you were talking of something

195

that triggered a familiar memory in Mrs Thackeray's mind. Something that would take her back to her life before. It would only take something of that nature to prompt her to thoughts of home.'

'I see, and there could be no other possible explanation?' I asked, hope now fading.

'No, I'm afraid not, madam.'

Seeing my disappointment he attempted to reassure me. 'Mrs Dickens, here at the asylum people are given that rare opportunity to live entirely for themselves, and themselves alone. Space to distance themselves from anything that causes pain or distress. As long as passion overturns reason, then the state of insanity will exist. If we all gave rein to every wild and unruly thought that passed through our mind and acted on it then we would all be in a state of insanity, it is our self-control and discipline that enables us to keep such things in their proper place. Life here has enabled Mrs Thackeray to quiet her mind, to shut out her pain and distress and regain some self-control. If anything were to intrude unlicensed into that space then her equanimity could be broken once again. I could not in all conscience permit her to risk that.'

'Then I shall have to trust you, Doctor, and try to believe that my friend can know no other happiness, beyond what she has found here.'

I left that dark study, saddened that I could do no more.

Later, lying in bed that night, the doctor's words came back to my mind, *'As long as passion overturns reason then a state of insanity exists.'* How often had my own passion overturned reason? How many times had I been suspicious of my husband's integrity and questioned the motives that lay behind his thoughtless words and actions? How often had I held myself back from exploding with rage over Georgie's unwanted intrusion in my life? So, if I was on the edge of reason, who was to blame? I, for not disciplining my boisterous thoughts, or others, for pushing me beyond what any woman should have to bear?

CHAPTER THIRTY-FOUR

September 1857
The Zoological Gardens, Regent's Park

Charles and the Macreadys had gone to look at the monkeys. Charles could not visit the zoological gardens without roaring at their antics and mimicking their behaviour. The children found it so amusing and Mr Macready urged him on in booming tones, but I did not enjoy the attention my husband's tomfoolery attracted at all, and wandered off to procure some ginger beer. Along with the Macreadys we had been accompanied by Augustus Egg, the painter. A small man with an apologetic face whose sentences frequently began, 'You are right, madam', or 'I couldn't agree more, madam', which became very irritating after a short while in his company. There seemed very little point in making conversation with such an agreeable man when he had no opposing point of view to make the conversation interesting. Charles, however, who always thought that he was right, could find no fault with a fellow who would not counter his infallibility.

Georgina, who went everywhere with us now, was once again in our party. Her figure had long since lost its childish roundness and in its place was a womanly sculpture. As the softness of her form had altered so too had the softness of her nature and its place was the coolness of marble, but Mr Egg – who had often visited our home – was never put off by this for one moment and it wasn't long before it became obvious that he was completely taken with her.

'She is a most marvellous woman, Mrs Dickens. Yes, that sister of yours is a veritable goddess of hearth and home. It is a lucky man who will make her his wife, yes it is.' he agreed with himself. He took out his handkerchief and mopped his brow as if just talking about her had caused him to become overwhelmed by the heat of his emotion. Georgie was not moved and remained coolly polite to him, but, undeterred, he trotted by her side throughout the morning and spoke to her with enthusiasm about the ornamental fountains and the variety of wild animals that filled the cages.

While fetching my ginger beer I noticed that Mr Egg had led my sister into the rose garden and I felt my pulse quicken and stood on my tiptoes to see above the hedging and observed that Mr Egg had removed his hat and was on bended knee. Would he really be so bold as to ask for my sister's hand? Georgie, however, had her back to me and to my frustration, I could not see her features nor guess her response. At last she and Mr Egg came out of the gardens and I adopted an air of nonchalance as I greeted them. Mr Egg remained his same agreeable self and Georgie remained as impassive as ever so I could detect nothing, but when Mr Egg excused himself and said that he was going to find Charles and the Macreadys, I could contain myself no longer.

'Well?' I hissed impatiently.

'Well, what?' Georgie replied unhelpfully.

'Mr Egg. Did he ask you?'

'He did.'

'Oh, Georgie!' I planted a dutiful kiss upon her cheek, saying, At last you are to be married.'

'But I did *not* accept him.'

The colour drained from my face. 'You did not accept him? Why ever not? Mr Egg is well placed in society, he has a handsome apartment in Bayswater. You wouldn't want for anything.'

'I want for nothing now,' Georgie replied with indifference.

'But you want to be wed, don't you? You can't mean to stay with Charles and I indefinitely. Of course, you are welcome to do so, but you must have plans of your own.'

Georgie stopped walking and faced me, her countenance filled with determination. 'Catherine, I know that my presence in your home is no longer welcomed by you, but whether you realize it or not, *you* need me, the children need me and Charles needs me. In life it is the destiny of some women to marry and the destiny of others to remain single. I have found my place in life and unless Charles asks me to leave, I shall stay as I am.'

Her destiny at that moment appeared to be that I would slap her, but I contained myself and resisted making a scene in public.

My eyes narrowed with resentment. 'I know what you are up to, Georgie, I am not ignorant of your plans.'

'I have no idea what you are talking about,' Georgie replied, with a toss of her head.

'You have plans to usurp me, don't you? And you will not give way until you have taken my place in my family's affections.'

Georgie sighed and prodded the ground firmly with her parasol. 'Catherine, the morning has already been made wearisome by the company of Mr Egg, I will not argue with you and I will ignore your cruel and unreasonable accusations.'

I heard the familiar call of my husband's voice and he waved as he approached with Mr Egg and the Macreadys in tow. I fell into a solemn silence as we rejoined them and Mr Egg continued to be so courteous and agreeable for the rest of the day, that no one could have guessed that he had just suffered a stinging rejection.

When it was time for us to leave, Mr Egg climbed into an open carriage with the Macreadys, Georgie accompanied the children, and Charles and I travelled home in our own brougham. Noticing my distraction, Charles who had been humming contentedly to himself, enquired, 'Is everything in order, my dear? You seem very quiet. Have you not enjoyed the day?'

My lips fixed together tightly as I eyed him with suspicion.

'Did you know that Augustus Egg had planned to propose to my sister today?'

'Did he, by Jove?' he chuckled. 'Brave fellow! And will she have him?'

I turned and looked out of the window. 'She will not.'

Charles roared, throwing his head back in amusement. 'I thought as much.'

' 'Tis no laughing matter, Charles. You must tell her. Tell her to marry him.'

His expression changed to one of sternness. 'I shall do no such thing. Your sister shall marry when and whom she pleases.'

I gripped Charles's arm in desperation. 'But can't you see what she is trying to do? She is trying to push me out, take over my life, my husband, my children. You must tell her to marry him. You must!'

Charles firmly removed my grip on his sleeve.

'I am damned if I will. You are becoming unhinged, Kate, and if you persist in this madness – and when I say madness, I mean madness – I will be forced to. . . . I shall have to . . . to call Dr Bell and . . . and—'

'Put me in an asylum, like Isabella Thackeray?' I spat.

'Don't be ridiculous, Kate, I never meant—'

'That would suit you very well, wouldn't it?'

'—any such thing. Now don't test me, Kate, I'm warning you—'

'To erase me from your life like some ill-chosen word in one of your novels.'

'—or I shall say something I—'

'To wipe me out as though I had never existed.'

'Yes!' he exploded unexpectedly. 'Yes, it *would* suit me. I should never have married you. There! I have said it at last. Let it be out in the open once and for all. We are ill matched and there are no two ways about it. You are fat, you are clumsy, you are lazy. Heavens above, woman, if it were not for Georgie the whole house would have come tumbling down around our ears and you would not even have noticed. How I have endured a life with you all this time is a miracle.'

He banged the roof of the cab and ordered the driver to stop.

'Where are you going?' I cried.

'I can no longer hold out under such provocation. I am walking home,' he said with weary regret, 'lest I say worse than has already been said.'

He got down from the cab and it pulled away leaving me to call after him. The cab continued through the grounds of The Regent's Park and I sat in a state of shock. Approaching the North Gate Bridge, the lake came into view and I signalled the driver to stop.

'Mr Dickens expressly ordered me to take you home, ma'am,' the driver said taking off his hat and scratching his head.

'I wish to walk,' I explained, taking a coin from my purse.

'It seems to me, ma'am, that this is not the sort of place for a lady like yourself to be out alone, and the day is almost drawing to a close. It will soon be dark.'

'I am not interested in your opinion, driver. Now take this for your trouble and leave me be. *Please!*'

The final word held a note of hysteria and, realizing he was beaten, the driver shrugged his shoulders and drove away. I wandered across the bridge and walked down to the edge of the lake where I stopped and stared down at the dark waters that danced hypnotically, repulsed by the moving reflection of my disjointed features.

'No wonder he despises me. I *am* ugly, I *am* useless.' I pulled and twisted my string of pearls in anguish.

A chorus of voices echoed within my head.

You are becoming unhinged, my dear.

I shall not marry anyone.

She is a fine woman, yes she is.

I shall have to call Dr Bell and . . . and. . . .

I twisted the pearls tighter and tighter and suddenly the necklace snapped and the pearls tumbled one by one into the water. I took another step closer to the water's edge.

'I would not go in there, ma'am. It is dirty and cold. Come. Come away with me and I will look after you.' His voice was gruff, as if it were full of city smog and he smelt of lamp oil. He wrapped his cloak around me and strangely I did not resist but leaned upon him, grateful of someone to bear the weight of all my troubles. Ladies dressed in all the colours of the sunset passed us by. They whispered to one another and acknowledged my companion, who nodded in return. In a moment the sun had faded, darkness fell and I remembered nothing more.

I awoke to the sound of a voice.

'Don't try to get up, ma'am, you are still very weak.'

I focused upon my surroundings and recognized them as my bedroom.

'Who brought me here?' I asked.

The voice answered and I realized that it was familiar too. It belonged to Dr Bell.

'The driver returned for you, Mrs Dickens, and a good thing it was that he did. I understand that you were about to take a very foolish step.'

He gently lifted my wrist, feeling for a pulse and put his other hand upon my brow. My eyes slowly flitted about the room and a feeling of sudden unease took hold of me. Something was not right. Something had changed. Charles's shaving brush and comb were gone from the washstand. I looked across the room and found that the place where his wardrobe stood was now vacant leaving behind only the marks on the wooden floor where it had been. His pocket book of Shakespeare which always sat upon his bedside table had disappeared too.

'Doctor?' I sat up, 'Where is my husband?'

He did not answer me, but instead reached into his old leather bag and began taking out a series of bottles each of which he squinted at, his eyesight not being what it used to be. Finally he settled on one. He peered at it intently, grunted with satisfaction and poured a few drops into a glass of water.

'Doctor, I asked you about my husband.'

'Yes,' he smiled kindly, 'I know, madam, but take this first – it will calm you a little.'

I gulped it down hurriedly, impatient to hear his explanation. The doctor took the glass from my hand and seeing my determined expression, knew that I would not be put off.

'Catherine,' he sighed, 'I have known you since you were born. I brought you into this world and placed you in your mother's arms, and if there were anything that I could do to spare you a moment's sadness then I would do it. I can only tell you as kindly as I can that I am afraid your husband has moved his possessions and set up his sleeping arrangements elsewhere in the house.'

I slowly took in the meaning of his words and then nodded with understanding. It appeared as though my sister had got what she wanted after all, my husband had no further use for me now, it was obvious. I reached for a hairbrush from my bedside table and began to brush my hair.

'Then I wish to see him, if you will call him, please.'

The doctor hesitated and I raised a conciliatory hand, 'I know, I know, I must not excite myself. You have my word. But I must know what his intentions are.'

My head began to spin a little and I realized that the sleeping draught was taking effect. The doctor left the room and returned presently with Charles at his side. He avoided my gaze, went straight to the fireplace and began warming his hands.

'Kate, if this has been some sort of attempt to win my sympathy, I can tell you now that it has not been successfully employed. I have told you before that I will not be held captive to a woman's emotions.'

'Charles, I may not have your sympathy, but I think that you owe me some sort of explanation as to what is going on.'

He turned from the fire and appealed to Dr Bell, 'How much does she know already?'

I leaned forward earnestly trying to catch his eye. 'I know that you have separated our sleeping arrangements. What *more* is there to know?'

Dr Bell looked at the glass at my bedside and nodded to Charles before leaving the room.

'Very well, then, I shall tell you.' Charles sighed.

'Catherine . . . Kate . . .' he began uncertainly. 'That you have been a loyal wife and mother is not called into question.' He cleared his throat. 'But I can no longer. . . . I am finding it difficult to. . . .' His hands fell to his side. 'Oh, Lord, I knew that this would not be easy. Kate, I must be honest and tell you that there . . . is someone else who now holds my affections.'

'I knew that Georgie would not be happy until she had won you to her side,' I remarked, bitterly.

He swivelled around abruptly, 'God, Kate, no! I could never. . . .'

He dropped down on to the end of the bed and held his head in his hands.

'Her name is Ellen Ternan. She is a talented young actress whom I met some months ago, after admiring her work. I never imagined then that my feelings for her would take on such strength. I've tried to stay away from her, God knows I have tried, but. . . .'

'Then what is to become of us?' I asked in bewilderment, trying to make sense of the sudden existence of this unknown woman. 'Or should I say, what is to become of *me*?'

Charles stood up and walked to the window. His voice took on a more assertive tone. 'The tenancy on this property comes to an end in three weeks' time. You may stay on until then, of course. And I will speak to your parents and ask if you might return to them until I find suitable accommodation for you.'

I fell back upon my pillow, taking in what had just been said and realizing that somehow I had always known that this day would come, that *she* would come – but in whose form I had not known. I had glimpsed her in the gentle nature of my sister Mary, in the charity of Miss Angela Burdett-Coutts, in the majesty of the Queen, in the soft voice of Consuela Swift, in the twisted mind of Madam de la Rue and in the cool authority of

Georgina. But how ironic it was that after a lifetime of suspicion, I had not suspected the existence of *this* woman in his affections at all. I had missed the signs completely.

'Do the children know about her?' I asked quietly.

'The children will do as I tell them to. It is none of their business.'

His harshness toward me I could accept, but his apparent disregard for the children's feelings aroused all of my maternal instincts.

'And will there be sufficient room for my children when you find this *suitable accommodation*?' My voice had become tinged with sarcasm.

Here I hit upon a raw note. Charles did not answer for a moment and then said with some caution, 'Georgie and I think ... Doctor Bell and I – think that it is best if they stay with me. You are not well at all. When I think what almost happened at the lake, I could not risk their safety.'

The feeling of anger that had lain dormant now rose to the surface, provoked beyond reason.

'I will not have my children living with you and that actress!' I spat.

Charles visibly bristled. 'There is no suggestion that Miss Ternan should ever live with me. I meant that Georgie should remain and look after them.'

'What a self-righteous hypocrite!' I screamed, snatching the glass from my bedside and hurling it at him.

The sound of breaking glass brought Dr Bell and Georgie bursting through the door.

Charles dabbed at his grazed temple with a handkerchief. 'The woman has injured me. I told you she was unstable!'

'Get her out.' I screamed, pointing at my sister. 'She must have known about this. She must have known what has been going on.' I wrestled with Dr Bell, who was trying to restrain me. 'Get her out! Get her out!'

Charles and my sister backed out of the room and I fell upon Dr Bell's shoulder and wept over all the wasted years of my life.

CHAPTER THIRTY-FIVE

October 1857
Tavistock House, London

Mama and Papa came.

'So, it has finally come to this has it, eh, Dickens? You would return my own daughter to me twenty-one years after I gave her into your hands for safe-keeping?'

'This is my house, Hogarth, and I would bid you to remember it. I am master here so do not challenge me in my own home.'

'Do ye hear that, John?' My mother interjected, sharply. 'He does no' want a challenge. Well, I'll give ye a challenge, laddie. We ken where ye came from and our daughter is too good for ye. We should ha' never let her go to anyone but a gentleman, and ye are not a gentleman. A blacking-factory boy, that's all ye are. Dressed up in dandy clothes, I grant ye, but a factory boy none the less.'

'Get out! Get out both of you! Out of my house!' Charles bellowed with increasing volume.

'Are ye coming, Georgie, or are ye staying here with this traitor?'

'I am staying with the children,' came Georgia's diplomatic return.

'Then ye are no longer a daughter of mine and I bid ye goodbye.'

Any hope of an amicable separation had from that moment

been destroyed. I think perhaps that Charles would have made it all as comfortable as any separation could hope to be, but my mother's words had altered his intentions completely; no one was going to label him the guilty party. My despatch from Tavistock House was carried out entirely by the servants, my bedroom furniture being unceremoniously loaded onto the back of a cart and driven off for storage at York Place. Alice and Emily helped me to pack up my personal belongings, and whilst Alice carried out her duties without emotion, Emily could not help but give way.

'Oh madam, to think that it should come to this. Who would have ever thought—?'

Alice looked at her sharply, 'Now, lassie, the mistress has no need of your tears, hurry y'self up with the packing!'

Charles stayed away at Gad's Hill, and arranged for Georgie to remove herself and the children to Broadstairs so that they should not see me go. I wandered through the rooms of the empty house, wondering what a woman could take with her that holds any meaning if she is to leave her children behind. In the weeks that followed the separation, the words that Charles had comforted me with – *'that you have been a loyal wife and devoted mother is not called into question'* – he himself now publicly called into question. He wrote to *The Times* and accused me of being a neglectful and uninterested mother, an incompetent wife, and that his separation from me was therefore entirely justified. That he was in fact praiseworthy in not doing it before now! Can you imagine how if felt to have that which had always been my reason for being, doubted, discredited and published before my friends, family and society?

Papa slapped shut the pages of his newspaper, folded it decisively and threw it onto the breakfast table.

'So the man has friends at *The Times*, does he? Well, I have friends too, friends who can publish facts that will make it clear to the whole world just what kind of a man Charles Dickens is!'

'Papa, please, I can't take any more animosity or ill-feeling. You will never win against him, Papa, never. As long as anyone dares to question his integrity, he will have the last word. Let it go now for all of our sakes, and let me try to build a life without him. He is much more likely to allow me to see the children if we don't antagonize him.'

Mama sniffed into her handkerchief, 'Oh, my poor girl. . . .'

Papa paced the morning room, 'It's not right, Catherine. I am your father, and I cannot allow anyone to treat you this way; and your sister, she has not acted with propriety or loyalty at all in staying on with the man.'

'Papa, I beg you, please do not meddle with him. For my sake?'

My father returned to the breakfast table and prodded the newspaper with his forefinger, 'For your sake, I will leave well alone, but if he and I should ever cross paths again. . . .'

Our friends could not help but be divided in their loyalties, for Charles had made it quite plain, you were either for him or against him. William was outraged at the news and was the first to visit me at York Place. He held out his hands in a warm greeting of support.

'Kate, my dear lady, I came as soon as I heard. I cannot imagine how he dares to treat you so treacherously. When I think of my poor Isabella and how I would give anything to be reunited with her; yet a man who could not wish for a more devoted wife chooses to turn his back on her in favour of some young actress. It is monstrous!'

'Dear William, please don't make an enemy of your old friend on my account.'

'No, no, Kate, I am your obedient servant from this day forth, and I shall have no further dealings with anyone who takes his side against you.'

'Then if you have any feeling for me, use your friendship with my husband to gain me access to the children. I do not ask for your loyalty or the loyalty of my friends, I only long to be reunited with my family.'

'I am afraid, Kate, that I am the wrong man to ask. I have

already severed all ties with him. Word of my personal opinion on your domestic circumstances has reached the newspaper; my disapproval of his actions is in the public domain. He will never receive me again, and other than not being able to assist you, I care not one damn!'

When I found a permanent place of residence in Gloucester Crescent – I could not complain of its location, so near to The Regent's Park – my eldest son, Charley, came to live with me. He had pleaded with his father to allow it, and with great perception convinced his papa that others would think well of him if he sanctioned it. The rest of the children were not permitted to visit, though, and I had been given no explanation for it.

'Why don't they come?' I asked Charley sadly, looking out of the window and seeming to see children wherever I looked, walking to the park with their mothers or nannies.

'They are confused, Mama, Aunt Georgie tells them that you are not well and that it would not be good for your health if they visited. Papa has told us all that his name is our passport to the future and that we would be foolish to separate ourselves from that.'

I squeezed his hand and reassured him that I understood.

'How *is* your father?'

Charley sighed. 'He works harder than ever, Mama. I fear that he will do himself great harm. He travels the length and breadth of the country performing his readings, he is at war with his publishers again – which has worn him down greatly – and now he is working on ideas for a weekly journal that he plans to edit. There are times when I speak to him and he looks right through me as though I am not even there.'

I could not help but ask then, 'Do you see *her* often when you visit him?'

Charley looked down at the floor in discomfort. 'Mama, it won't do you any good to ask about such things.'

'Sometimes, my love, I think imagining it all is far worse. Do you know that when your father made her existence known to me, he wanted me to meet her just to prove to the newspapers that there was nothing more than friendship between them! I have done many things in my life to salve his conscience, but what he asked of me then was too unbearable to contemplate. Yet, I wonder about her all the same. Please tell me what you know.'

'She is very young, Mama. It is quite embarrassing, but she is polite to us all and is always accompanied by her mother when she visits. But I do not believe that Father is truly happy. I think he carries a great sense of guilt, a feeling that his own happiness has come at the expense of others.'

'I am not bitter, my love, I had twenty-one wonderful years with your papa and even if I had known what the outcome was going to be, I do not think that I would have done anything any differently. My only wish is to be reunited with your brothers and sisters – if only there was a way.'

Some days later I received an unexpected visit from Miss Burdett-Coutts and it seemed that she had news of a solution to my difficulties.

She took of her gloves and kissed me on either cheek. 'I'm so sorry, my dear, that I have not come before but I trust that you received my letters of support? Charles is still so sensitive about the issue between the two of you and I dare not risk any harm to our charity work together by upsetting him. It's the girls I'm thinking of, you understand?'

'Of course, Angela, I know that your work at the home is very important to you.'

Emily brought a tray into the sitting room, placed it on the small table at the side of my chair and, while I poured out the tea, Miss Burdett-Coutts made the reason for her visit plain. 'Now you must not let Charles know that you heard mention of this from me, but I have some news for you. While visiting Gad's Hill last Sunday, I overheard Charles saying to your sister that if he could be sure that the children would have no contact with their grandparents, then he would consider allowing you to see them. My dear, if you were to write him and suggest this as your own idea, it may go in your favour.'

I absorbed the meaning of her words: could it be that there was hope? And for the first time in many months I took on a sense of lightness, a feeling that happiness was not entirely out of my reach. William had written to me and made reference to the recent Matrimonial Causes Act, which he felt might give me a way to see the children, but I knew that if I faced Charles in court and tried to prove his guilt, he would use every means in his power against me. He would stamp on whatever hope I had with absolute vehemence and extinguish it completely. But if I were to try the suggestion being voiced to me now, it might find favour with him, and cause him to relent. I looked at the clock on the mantelpiece, its pendulum swinging back and forth, and got to my feet.

'There is not a moment to lose, madam, I will put pen to paper with all haste.'

'Then, my dear, I pray God bless you in doing so.' Witnessing my great urgency in searching the bureau for my writing implements, she left her tea and rose to leave.

There was no formal reply from Charles to my appeal, no humble acknowledgement that perhaps he had been too severe with me in former times, or that he appreciated the sacrifice that my own parents would be making in this matter. But when I received word from Katie that she and her sister were to visit, never mind! My dear girls were coming to see me and every moment that passed until they stepped over my threshold was a moment too long.

CHAPTER THIRTY-SIX

1857
Gloucester Crescent, London

'Married? To Mr Collins? No, Katie, you cannot be in earnest? He is such a strange little man, with the most immoderate habits.'

'No Mama, you have misunderstood, it is Mr *Charles* Collins that I mean to wed, Mr Wilkie's brother.'

'But that is just as bad, my dear. Mary won't you tell her she will be making a terrible mistake? The man is as dull as ditchwater.'

'Nonsense, Mama,' Katie snapped. 'He is a little reserved I grant you, but he is such a wonderful artist.'

'And what has your father to say about this?'

Katie did not reply, but her eyes blazed with resentment, angry that I had touched upon a weakness in her argument.

'There! Just as I thought, your papa has doubts too, doesn't he? Tell me if I'm wrong.' I placed my hand beneath her resolute chin and gently lifted it. 'Katie, you have too much of your father in you to live with such a man as Charles Collins. He will bore you; he will exasperate you. Katie, one failed marriage in the Dickens family is enough, don't you think?'

Katie pushed my hand away and paced the room with irritation. 'Mama, are you saying that just because you and Papa are opposites that Mr Collins and I cannot hope to be happy

212

because we are different?'

'I am saying that I think that you would be better suited to someone younger, someone who can match your own enthusiasm for life. Why are you in such a hurry, anyway?'

She had her back to me, her arms folded in defiance and then I understood.

'Have you and your father been arguing again? You have, haven't you? Oh, Katie, this is not the answer at all. You will be running away from unhappiness in one place only to find it in another. Please, Katie, if you will not change your mind, then at least reflect on the idea of this marriage for a little longer, you are only eighteen after all.'

Her arms remained folded in a gesture of wilfulness, and I appealed to her sister.

'Mary?'

Mary's voice was soft and full of conciliation. 'Mama, you should know by now that when Katie has decided, no one will alter her opinion.'

An invitation to the wedding never arrived, and I was unsure who had most wished me absent, my prejudiced husband or my obstinate daughter.

When Charley returned home from the celebrations and found me sitting alone, he could not contain his indignation and anger.

'How can they treat you this way, Mama? I could hardly bear to be there, knowing that you were here on your own and that Papa had invited that awful young woman, along with her sister and mother in your place.'

'There, there, my love. It is done now and no amount of bitterness will undo it. I am more concerned for Katie than for myself. I only hope that she does not regret her hasty decision, but I fear that she will.'

Charley, who appeared to have already had a little too much too drink, poured himself a glass of whisky, and took a large gulp.

'Well, Papa put on his usual façade, entertaining the guests with his tricks, dancing and sketches, but when they had all gone, I found him at the bottom of the garden, crying over Katie's departure and burning his entire collection of letters in the fire basket.'

'His letters! But there is a lifetime of memories recorded amongst many of them. Why would he do such a thing?'

'I have no idea, Mama.' He gulped at the whisky again. 'And, to be honest, I no longer care. I am ashamed to call him my father.'

'No, my love, you must never say that. Your father has his faults, but he is still a fine man. Look at the wonderful, charitable acts that he has performed throughout his life. I never give up hope, Charley, that your father will repent of his mistakes and that we will be reunited again. You must be patient with him.'

11th June 1870
Gad's Hill Place, Kent

The days, months and years passed, and my life continued to be inextricably linked to all that my husband said and did. I began the recounting of our life together in this journal, feeling that by retracing my steps I might live it all again. I read all of his works, attended many of his readings and performances, and his photograph stood in a frame, placed at my bedside. From time to time he would write to me in a polite manner and enquire after my health, and whether my way of life was all that it had been.

Charley was now married and employed in the offices of his father's magazine, Francis and Walter were in India, Sydney a midshipman in the navy, Alfred was in Australia, Henry at Cambridge and young Edward finally coming to the end of his schooling.

When old Mrs Dickens passed away, (and sadly Fred the following year), I received formal notification from Charles that the funerals had taken place. He sent word when Georgie was taking the sea air in France to ease her heart trouble, and when the newspapers reported upon the most terrible train crash at Staplehurst, and that a famous author was shaken but unhurt, he assured me via a telegraph that Mr Charles Dickens was quite well and that I had no need to enquire of him further.

My dear friend, William Thackeray finally passed away and twelve years after Charles and I separated, the day that I prayed would never come, arrived.

The click of the sitting room door being opened roused me from an afternoon nap in my chair.

'Hello, my love, I was not expecting your visit today.' I smiled, lifting my head from the wing of the chair.

Charley's face was pinched into an expression far too serious for one of such handsome features and immediately I knew that something was not right.

'What is it, my love?'

Charley knelt down at the side of my chair, and took my hand. 'It is Father, Mama, he is very ill. Aunt Georgie has sent a telegram; she thinks that you should come straight away.'

'Have you seen him?' I asked, twisting at my necklace.

'He is very confused, Mama. I think that you will have to be very strong.'

We travelled in silence to Gad's Hill and I looked out of the window, seeing nothing, hearing nothing, only thinking of him. Perhaps I knew that it would be too late, that Charles would no longer be there when I arrived, but still nothing prepared me for the sight that was to greet me at Gad's Hill. Katie, Mary and Georgie were sitting on the steps leading up to the front door, clutching one another and weeping. Mary and Kate sprang to their feet immediately and ran to embrace me.

'Oh Mama, Mama, he has gone!'

I felt as if my legs would give way from under me, but Katie took my arm and led me into the house and to the room where he lay.

'I will leave you alone with him for a while, Mama.'

He slept on a narrow velvet couch in the drawing room. In all our years together I had never seen him so quiet and still, with such a look of rest and ease about him, with such patient serenity. I wondered how this worn out body could have contained the restless and vital force that had been his. The June sunshine streamed through the windows and filled the room with reflected brilliance, and I thought how Heaven must be just as matchless in its beauty. If only I could be reunited with him now, with my youth and beauty restored, that I could be all to him in eternity that I had not been in this life. I knelt down at his side and lifted his hand to my face.

'Charles, I am so sorry that I . . . disappointed you.' Even now I could hardly bring myself to utter the word 'failed'.

'I tried my best, truly I did.'

I realized with despair that we no longer shared the same world, and any hope of reconciliation was now extinguished. I could not imagine that I would never see him again, that he had gone forever.

The door opened quietly and Katie's voice asked softly, 'Are you all right, Mama?'

Brushing aside my tears, I nodded and replaced her father's hand at his side. Seeing me struggle, she crossed the room, slipped her arm through mine and helped me to my feet.

'He looks so peaceful, Mama, don't you think? He had such a fear of being idle and yet, I think that if he had lived much longer, he would have worked until he'd driven himself out of his mind.'

I put a finger to my lips, ever mindful of her father's great pride, and led her out into the conservatory. The heavy scent of the garden permeated the air and we sat down, glad of the sun's warmth on our grief-weary bodies.

'Papa was reminiscing a few days ago about old times, when

we were all together, and he sounded so full of guilt and regret. He said that he wished he had been a better father, a better human being.'

I placed my hand reassuringly upon my daughter's.

'Your father *was* a wonderful human being, Katie; it's just that sometimes I think he forgot the distinction between truth and fiction. He treated us as though we were all characters in his books, as if he could control our thoughts, and words and actions.'

'But you have forgiven him, Mama, haven't you?'

'Now that he has gone, my love, all our differences seem so unimportant. During those years without him there were times when I both loved and resented him, and yet I never stopped hoping that he would alter his opinion of me and call me back to his side.'

'You know that you will be welcome at the funeral, don't you Mama?'

I smiled sadly. 'No, my love, I will not be there. It is him they will come to see. I have determined to remember him in my own quiet manner.'

I stood up and walked out into the garden. Looking back toward the house, I could see him now in my mind's eye working away on some new idea, and I thought back to the first time that I met him and to the day when my father introduced us.

To the day when my life changed from the ordinary to the remarkable.

APPENDIX

Chapter One
There are a number of sources which describe an occasion when Dickens once jumped through a sitting-room window and danced the hornpipe, before jumping back out of the window again to the surprise of the guests. I have used this as the setting for the first meeting between Charles and Catherine.

George Hogarth was a music critic and journalist for the *Morning Chronicle*, and was in time appointed as the editor for the *Evening Chronicle*. Mr John Black was the editor at the *Morning Chronicle*, and Sir John Easthope – the proprietor. Thomas Anderson, Dr Bell and Elizabeth George are entirely fictitious characters.

At this time Charles Dickens was residing with his brother, Frederick at Furnival's Inn and although he knew Thomas Mitten he did not meet John Forster until 1836.

Chapter Two
In the spring of 1829 Dickens met and fell in love with Maria Beadnell, but her father, the banker George Beadnell, did not favour the match and the relationship ended.

Chapter Three
Dickens's older sister Fanny, was an accomplished singer and her characteristics as they appear in this novel are completely fictionalized. Letitia and Harriet were Dickens's younger sisters,

and Frederick and Augustus his younger brothers. Only Frederick and Fanny are referred to in the novel. Catherine Dickens had a sister, Helen, and a brother, who are both omitted from the novel.

Chapter Four
Mary Hogarth was to live with Catherine and Charles after their marriage until she died in May 1837 at the age of 17.

Chapter Five
The date of Charles Dickens's marriage to Catherine was 2 April 1836. The ceremony took place at St Luke's Church, Chelsea. How Dickens felt about his family's presence at the ceremony is unknown, but it is a well-known fact that his father would ask his son for money, and that Dickens did not like his mother to dance.

Chapter Six
A letter of agreement to write the novel *Gabriel Varden* was given to the publisher, John Macrone, by Dickens. There is uncertainty around whether Dickens remembered doing this, but when he withdrew from writing the novel he reluctantly accepted £100 for the entire copyright of both series of *Sketches by Boz* as a form of compensation to Macrone.

Chapter Seven
Dickens and Mary purchased the small table as a gift for Catherine as recorded in his diary on 6 January 1838. A party to celebrate the success of *Pickwick* was held on 31 March 1838 at Furnival's Inn.

Chapter Eight
Mrs Rozawich and her daughter, Esther, are fictional characters.

Chapter Nine
Dickens worked on dramatizations with both Mr John Braham and Mr John Harley at the St James's Theatre during the year 1838.

Mary Hogarth died at 48 Doughty Street in May 1837. Dickens did instruct his lawyer to change his will to indicate his wish to be buried in the same plot, but this was made impractical upon the death of Mary's brother a short while later. Dickens insisted that Mary's room and possessions remain untouched.

Chapter Ten
Dickens and his family spent many summers at Broadstairs in Kent.

Chapter Eleven
On their second wedding anniversary, Charles and Catherine stayed at the Star and Garter Inn, Richmond, and were joined by Forster after a few days. The account of the small boy who wrote to Dickens is true.

Chapter Twelve
In 1838 Dickens opened an account at Coutts and Company and was introduced to Angela Burdett-Coutts by Mr Edward Marjoribanks. The well-recorded argument between Dickens and Forster took place in 1840 in the presence of the Macreadys and Catherine. The cause of the argument is unknown but it resulted in Catherine leaving the room in tears.

Chapter Thirteen
In 1846 Miss Burdett-Coutts and Dickens began work on an idea to open a home for fallen women which later became known as Urania Cottage. Sir Robert Bradbury-Kent is a fictional character.

Chapter Fourteen
In December 1839 the Dickens family moved to Devonshire Terrace.

Chapter Fifteen
During the time that the Dickens family resided at Devonshire Terrace, Dickens purchased a raven whom he named 'Grip'.

Chapter Sixteen
In February 1839 it came to the attention of Dickens, via his publishers Chapman and Hall, that his father – John Dickens – had applied to them for a loan. At a later date John Dickens forged bills with his son's name on and also counterfeited his work for sale.

Chapter Seventeen
Early in the year of 1840, Dickens declared to his friends that he was in love with Queen Victoria. In July 1840, Dickens witnessed the hanging of Courvoiser at Newgate Prison; he was accompanied by the artist, Daniel Maclise, and his brother-in-law Henry Burnett. Dickens subsequently began a campaign for the abolition of public hangings.

Chapter Eighteen
Eleanor Picken, also known as 'Emma' and as Mrs Emma Christian, stayed with the Dickens family in Broadstairs. She was related to Mrs Smithson, whose characteristics I have fictionalized. The account of Dickens picking Eleanor up and dancing in the waves is recorded in her own account of the episode.

Chapter Twenty
In June 1841, Catherine and Charles visited Scotland, where they stayed at the Royal Hotel, Edinburgh and visited Catherine's former home. Catherine escaped from the runaway carriage before it ended up in the water.

Chapter Twenty-one
In November 1841, Dickens began to have thoughts of travelling to America and asked Catherine to accompany him. The children were looked after partly by his brother Frederick and by the McCreadys. By now, Fanny Dickens was married to Mr Henry Burnett, a musician.

Chapter Twenty-two
Charles and Catherine travelled on *The Britannia* and had great
fears about whether they would arrive safely as the crossing was
rough. Thomas and Consuela Swift are fictitious characters but
Dickens's fleeting infatuation with Mrs Swift is based on his
feelings for Mrs Francis Colden of New York.

The route taken by Charles and Catherine Dickens is recorded
in Dickens's own journal – *American Notes*. The account at
Niagara Falls is recorded by several of Dickens's biographers.

Chapter Twenty-three
In spring 1839, Frederick, aided by his brother, began work at the
Treasury where he was employed for at least the next twenty
years. Frederick Dickens married Anna Weller, sister to
Christina, a pianist; the account of his affair with Christina is
wholly fictitious. In the late 1850s Frederick's marriage to Anna
collapsed under financial strain and allegations of adultery.

Chapter Twenty-four
The Dickens family travelled to Genoa in June 1844 and became
friends with Emile and Augusta de la Rue. Catherine was so
jealous of the relationship between Charles and Augusta that she
ordered her husband to break off the friendship.

Chapter Twenty-five
It was probably around the autumn of 1842 that Georgina
Hogarth came to live with the Dickens family on a permanent
basis.

Chapter Twenty-six
Count d'Orsay and Lady Blessington lived at Gore House
together until April 1849, after which they fled to France to
escape their creditors. Lady Blessington died in June 1849 and
Count d'Orsay in August 1852.

The Dickens's seventh child, Sydney, was born in April 1847.
In the late summer of 1847, both Catherine and Charles returned

from Paris to be near to their son, Charley, when he became ill with scarlet fever, but Catherine was not allowed to be in his company due to her pregnancy.

Fanny Dickens was taken ill and died from consumption in September 1848.

Chapter Twenty-seven
In March 1838, William and Isabella Thackeray's baby daughter, Jane, died. After the birth of her third child in 1840, Isabella succumbed to puerperal depression and tried to drown herself in the sea in September of that year. For the following two years she was cared for professionally in England, and after that was confined to a home in Paris, where she remained until 1893. There are no recorded meetings between her and Catherine Dickens.

Chapter Twenty-eight
Peter Rozawich and his wife are fictional characters.

Chapter Twenty-nine
John and Elizabeth Dickens lived under the care of a surgeon, Dr Davey, and his wife in Russell Square. John Dickens died in March 1851 as a result of an operation for the removal of bladder stones which he endured without anaesthetic. Not many days after his father's funeral, Dickens spent the night in the cell of a police station.

Chapter Thirty
Towards the end of 1850, Dickens wrote about the death of Dora Spenlow, a character in the novel *David Copperfield*. His own daughter, Dora, died in April 1851. Forster travelled to Malvern to break the news to Catherine.

Chapter Thirty-one
In November 1851, the Dickens family moved to Tavistock Square. In March of that year Dickens was introduced to Wilkie Collins through the artist, Augustus Egg.

Chapter Thirty-two

In 1855, Dickens became reacquainted with Maria Beadnell who was now married to Mr Henry Winter. They had two daughters. Henry Winter was a businessman, but there is no record of his being a gambler. The character, Flora Finching, in Dickens's novel *Little Dorrit* is said to be based on Maria Beadnell.

Chapter Thirty-four

In 1857, Augustus Egg proposed to Georgina Hogarth. She refused him, preferring instead to stay on in the Dickens household. Dickens met the actress Ellen Ternan in August 1857 and Charles and Catherine separated in May 1858.

Chapter Thirty-five

Catherine left Tavistock House after the separation, and moved to Gloucester Crescent where she lived with her eldest son, Charley. In July 1860, Katie Dickens married Mr Charles Collins, the younger brother of Wilkie Collins. The marriage was childless.

Chapter Thirty-Six

On 11 June 1870 Charles Dickens passed away at his home at Gad's Hill. Much against his preferences for a quiet funeral, the service was held at Westminster Abbey. His wife, Catherine, did not attend.